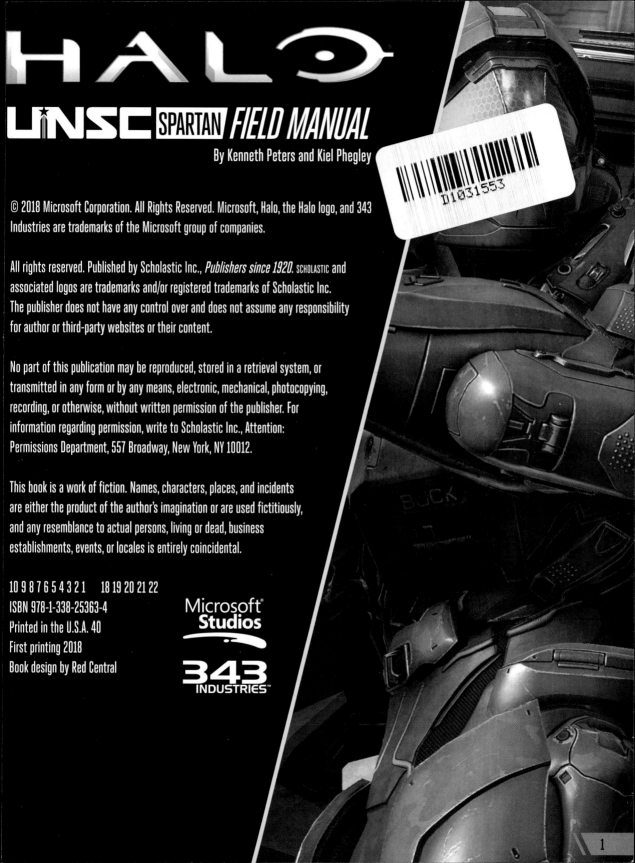

# HALO

## UNSC SPARTAN FIELD MANUAL

By Kenneth Peters and Kiel Phegley

All rights reserved. Published by Scholastic Inc., *Publishers since 1920.* SCHOLASTIC and associated logos are trademarks and/or registered trademarks of Scholastic Inc. The publisher does not have any control over and does not assume any responsibility for author or third-party websites or their content.

10 9 8 7 6 5 4 3 2 1    18 19 20 21 22
ISBN 978-1-338-25363-4
Printed in the U.S.A. 40
First printing 2018
Book design by Red Central

Microsoft® Studios

343 INDUSTRIES™

# DUTY.
# HONOR.
# SACRIFICE.

These are the cornerstones of the Spartan Code. For decades, the United Nations Space Command has relied on these powerful super-soldiers to protect the interests of the Unified Earth Government across hundreds of colony worlds, and the Code is what drives every Spartan to excel in the arts of war and diplomacy. Upholding the Spartan Code is never easy, but when the lives of billions are in the balance, it is all that stands between victory and annihilation. Legends have stayed true to the Spartan Code, and now you are asked to continue that legacy. This is not a path for the weak of heart.

This manual is designed to introduce you to the Spartan program and our mission as part of the United Nations Space Command. You will be joining as a fourth-generation Spartan, but in these pages you will learn about the history of the legends who have spearheaded the technologies and tactics you use today, and what to expect in the future now that you have completed initial training and joined your fellow Spartans in the common defense of humanity.

# UNSC SPARTAN-IV PROGRAM
# ENLIST
## DO YOU HAVE WHAT IT TAKES?

# CONTENTS

# PART 01
# INTRODUCTIONS

FROM: INFINITY Operations Center
SUBJ: Spartan Operations Update

## ///PRIORITY ALPHA PRIVATE MESSAGE///

Welcome Aboard, Spartan.

I apologize for the brevity, Spartan, but the UNSC INFINITY has recently finished its refit and we are preparing to deploy within the next 24 hours. Standard onboarding and orientation is canceled, and you are to report immediately to Spartan Miller, who will be your Mission Handler for the duration. Our next operation will take us to the fringe world of Kamchatka, and you will be in the second wave of the assault. If the analysts at ONI are right, a victory there will give us the edge we need to take out the largest of the Covenant factions and win the UNSC some much-needed breathing room. You signed up to take risks and make a mark on history, and this is your chance.

On a more personal note, you may have impressed High Command with your medals and letters of recommendation, but as far as I'm concerned, your record was wiped clean the instant you boarded the INFINITY and came under my command. That said, you have the full support of myself, Captain Lasky, and every Spartan on board. Good luck, Spartan, and see you at the next victory parade.

Sarah Palmer (65287-98303-SP)

Spartan Commander, UNSC INFINITY (INF-101)

# UNSC INFINITY

FROM: Spartan Thorne
TO: Spartan Field Manual

Welcome to the UNSC INFINITY, Spartan. I'm Spartan Thorne, and I've been asked by Commander Palmer to be your point of contact for orientation. I've seen your record, but take it from me that your time on the INFINITY will be the most eventful and dangerous of your entire UNSC career.

To prepare for our upcoming missions I've amended your Spartan Field Manual with some personal notes and lessons learned, because if there's one thing that Commander Palmer insists on, it's being prepared. Spartan Hoya always says, "No one really reads the manual," but I'm hoping that, with the help of myself and Spartan Grant, you'll be ready for a pop quiz by Commander Palmer within the week.

Spartan Thorne (83920-91083-GT)

Fireteam Leader - Fireteam Majestic

# UNSC INFINITY

FROM: Spartan Grant
TO: Spartan Field Manual

And I'm Spartan Grant, who you may remember from your tour of duty back on Passage. Fireteam Majestic provided support for your team in that strike against an "unguarded" Covenant arms depot. Yeah, not so unguarded as it turned out . . . Anyway, glad to see that they managed to patch you back together after that. And congratulations on making good on that promise to become a Spartan!

Landing on Requiem, engaging with that Forerunner tech, fighting the Covenant, seeing the Promethean Knights up close . . . it's made me realize that there's a lot more going on than they tell us in our official briefings. The way I see it, if one scrap of information in here helps us make better decisions on the battlefield—if it helps save one more life—then this was all worth it. I'm adding some secrets I've found in the parts of the UNSC intranet that they don't share with you at boot camp or the Spartan training campus; some of which may—technically—be above your clearance level.

Oh, and a friendly bit of advice: Don't go spilling these secrets to Spartan Madsen. He can't keep his mouth shut about anything.

Stay safe, Spartan.

Spartan Grant (95984-78393-TG)

Spartan - Fireteam Majestic

# WELCOME ABOARD THE UNSC *INFINITY*!

While aboard the UNSC *Infinity*, you are a guest of Captain Lasky and the ship's crew. As such, it is important to observe the traditional Navy customs and courtesies. Should you have any questions or concerns about proper shipboard behavior, or wish to know more about naval tradition, the AI ship director, Roland, is more than happy to be of assistance.

## PERMISSION TO COME ABOARD

Boarding a UNSC warship is a ceremony, not a formality. When you return to the *Infinity* and tell the officer on deck (OOD), "I request permission to come aboard, sir," you are really telling them that your skills are at their service. The OOD may only offer a curt, "Very well," but this adherence to tradition should act as the basis for your interaction with the Navy personnel you'll be serving with for months on end. Respect those on board, and they will respect you in turn.

## RIGHT OF WAY IS THE BEST WAY

First and foremost, it is the obligation of Spartans to make way for the crew and not impede their work in any way. Even in instances where you might outrank ship personnel, their vital function on the vessel should be respected at all times.

## ATTENTION!

It is not appropriate to salute Navy officers with the left hand. You are not expected to salute when wearing Mjolnir armor, but do use formal greetings when encountering superior officers.

## KEEP THE *INFINITY* SHIPSHAPE

All personnel on a Navy ship are expected to participate in working parties, which includes assisting in routine maintenance or providing labor during critical ship replenishment operations. Spartan Commander Palmer is responsible for ensuring that Spartans participate, and you are ordered to display the utmost professionalism in the course of your assigned duties, no matter how menial they may appear.

# UNSC INFINITY

## MEMORANDUM

From: T. Lasky, CAPT
Reply to Captain, UNSC INFINITY
Attn of: Spartan Miller

To: Spartan Force Replenishment Group Victor
– 17 OCT 2558
Subj: WELCOME ABOARD

### ///WELCOME ABOARD///

Spartan,

Congratulations on your assignment to INF-101 INFINITY, flagship of the UNSC Navy! Our mission is vital to the security of the Unified Earth Government, and you are vital to our success. You are currently pending assignment to a Spartan Fireteam, and you will be assigned to general security duties until you are transferred to an open billet. I am informed by Spartan Commander Sarah Palmer that a schedule for training and orientation has already been prepared, and that you are to review your Spartan Field Manual for information on this ship, its crew, and information relevant to your upcoming missions.

INFINITY is the largest and most powerful vessel ever employed by humanity and currently serves as the ceremonial flagship for the UNSC Navy, as well as the lead ship in the newly established Expeditionary Strike Group ONE fleet. Built to stand toe-to-toe with the Covenant's assault carriers, the INFINITY measures over five kilometers long and is fitted with more firepower than entire fleets of older UNSC warships. It is also home to over 17,000 of the finest men and women in the United Nations Space Command. This ship is their home, and they will be your friends, neighbors, and support staff for the duration of your deployment. Their professionalism and fighting spirit is inspiring, and you could not ask for a more brilliant crew to support you in the battles to come. As a Spartan stationed aboard the INFINITY, you will be an ambassador for the ship as well as a warfighter and will conduct yourself in a manner befitting your training and legacy of excellence as we conduct strategically important missions for the UNSC, both within human space and in unexplored frontiers.

INFINITY is currently conducting high-tempo, multi-threat combat operations as part of *Expeditionary Strike Group One* (ESG 1). We are preparing to depart the Sol to assault a Covenant staging area in the Caspar system as part of Operation: ANCHORITE. As you already know, combat operations are expected to begin as soon as we exit slipspace, in less than a week. With the recent news of attacks on the Oban and Ursa IV, I know every Spartan is on edge and ready for a fight. Your time will come.

Roland, INFINITY's ship director and command AI, has made arrangements for your living quarters and pay accounting. Spartan Miller has been assigned as your temporary Mission Handler, and all questions related to your temporary duty schedule are to be made through him. However, I have an open-door policy for every member of my crew, and Roland will be more than happy to schedule an appointment if you have any questions or concerns. For now, get some rest, tour the ship, talk to the crew, and take this opportunity to review your basic skills before the shooting starts.

On behalf of the crew of the INFINITY, I welcome you aboard!

CAPTAIN THOMAS LASKY
Commanding Officer, UNSC INFINITY

**RANK:** Captain
**SERVICE NUMBER:** 98604-72690-TL
**HEIGHT:** 1820 mm (5ft 11in)
**WEIGHT:** 76.7 kg (169 lbs)
**BIRTHWORLD:** Mars
**DATE OF BIRTH:** August 15, 2510

# CAPTAIN THOMAS LASKY

Thomas Lasky is a proven and remarkable leader, deeply talented in a variety of naval tactics, whether in the direction of UNSC flagship INFINITY or the deployment of military assets. Lasky has proven himself to be a courageous and faithful leader, one who values the lives of his crew.

Today, Captain Lasky applies lessons learned over his decades of exemplary naval service to his stewardship of our flagship. His priority as INFINITY captain is making strategic command decisions that defend human life and maintain fleet integrity at all costs. But he also has helped carve out a unique place for Spartan-IVs as frontline combatants wherever danger may rear its head. Should time and duty allow, Captain Lasky has allocated part of his busy schedule to personally meet and greet every Spartan-IV who comes aboard the INFINITY. Until then, the Captain wishes to relay that he has the utmost faith and confidence in your abilities, and you can be assured that you have the full backing of both himself and the crew of the INFINITY in your missions.

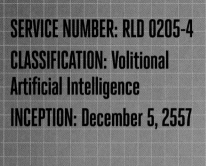

**SERVICE NUMBER: RLD 0205-4**

**CLASSIFICATION: Volitional Artificial Intelligence**

**INCEPTION: December 5, 2557**

# ROLAND

Our AI ship director, Roland, can answer any questions you may have about navigating the ship, work schedule assignments, or even join you for a game of chess. His interface avatar is that of a veteran World War II pilot, which perfectly captures his bravado and outstanding piloting ability. Roland has administrative authority over all AIs aboard the ship, including the expert systems and software constructs who manage various compartments of the INFINITY. As the ship's director he is a trusted and vital member of the command crew, and his orders are to be obeyed as if they were given by Captain Lasky or Spartan Commander Palmer.

## GRANT

Roland is tethered to his data processing and storage unit, located on the bridge, but he can monitor the entire ship from there, and display his cheeky little avatar at any holoterminal if he wants face time. If his housing is destroyed, we're in big trouble, as Roland is the only AI on this ship who has the skill and dedicated subprocesses needed to keep the INFINITY going. As he is a military construct, Spartans do have authority to take him out if he shows signs of rampancy (a personality fragmentation that begins seven years after creation), but none of us are looking forward to that possibility.

## THORNE

For all his annoying personality quirks, Roland really is a member of our family on the INFINITY. I know you've had bad experiences with AIs in the past, but Roland is different, and if you disrespect him, you'll be answering to a lot of angry Spartans.

# UNSC INFINITY LAYOUT

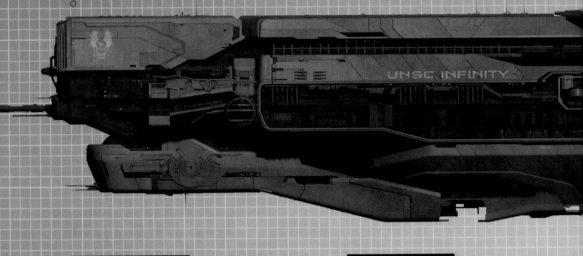

## BOOTS ON THE GROUND

For the duration of our mission, 5,400 Marines are stationed aboard the *Infinity* and ready for immediate deployment. They are grouped into five independent task forces, each with infantry, armor, and air support.

## A FLEET UNTO ITSELF

The *Infinity* can transport up to ten Anlace- or Strident-class frigates within its internal hangar bays. Each Anlace-class frigate is 372 meters in length. That is more than two Seattle Space Needles placed end-to-end!

# SPECIFICATIONS

**CLASS:** *Infinity*-class Supercarrier

**HULL CODE:** INF-101

**CREW:** 11,300

**TROOPS:** 7,500

**MASS:** 907 million metric tons

**MANEUVER DRIVE:** XR2 Boglin Fields S81/X fusion drive (primary)

**TRANSLIGHT ENGINE:** Mark X Macedon/Z-Prototype #78720HDS Revision 2.1

**ARMAMENT:** 4×CR-03B Series 8 Magnetic Accelerator Cannons; 350×M42 Archer missile pods; 250×M75 Rapier missile pods; 190×M97 Lance missile pods; 500×M96 Howler missile pods; 85×M85 Scythe anti-aerospace turrets; 10×Mark 2551 Onager MAC turrets; 830×M965 Fortress point defense guns

**ENERGY SHIELDING:** Misriah Armory MG-44N Heavy Dispersal Field Generators

## HEAVY METAL

The *Infinity* masses 907 million metric tons. That is equivalent to 10,000 21st-century wet-navy aircraft carriers!

## SUPERCARRIER

The *Infinity* is 5,694 meters (18,682 feet) in length. This makes it slightly larger than the Covenant Assault Carrier, itself one of the largest ships ever seen.

## ADVANCED TRANSLIGHT ENGINE

The faster-than-light slipspace engine of the *Infinity* is built around a Forerunner drive core recovered during the Covenant War. This drive is what makes the *Infinity* one of the fastest ships in the fleet, despite its size.

# KEY LOCATIONS

## ARMOR BAY

The Armor Bay is where you can select your Mjolnir suit and accessories, and where your armor can be repaired and stored after mission. It also acts as the maintenance hub for all Spartan tech and special equipment. The technical staff are there to ensure that both you and your Mjolnir suit operate at peak performance.

## MEMORIAL PARK

The *Infinity* comes with additional amenities rarely seen on UNSC warships. Perhaps the most impressive of these is the Memorial Park atrium, a lush, self-contained biosphere that replicates the feeling of life on planet for those soldiers who are rarely able to make it home. Spartans are known for their singular-focus on mission readiness, but we recommend finding time for relaxation in designated recreational facilities. Just as you rest y muscles, resting your mind is integral to battle readiness.

## HANGAR BAY

The *Infinity* has eight primary hangars from which dropships and other transports can launch and return to ship. Larger bays are used for replenishment by more sizable cargo transports and as docking ports for waste, water, and fuel transfer. Spartans will quickly become acquainted with the ship's mass deployment bays and dropship landing zones, as it is not uncommon for mission briefings and prep ops to happen on the move your transport. These areas are always busy, with fast-moving vehicles a cargo. Be mindful of your surroundings and make way for crew members.

## SPARTAN TOWN

Aboard the *Infinity*, you will be assigned quarters in "Spartan Town," a limited-access area only accessible to Spartan-IVs and support personnel. Post-augmentation, your need for sleep will be reduced, but you will be provided with many opportunities for socialization outside of combat training. Note that personal effects are to be kept to a minimum, and that regular inspections of both individual and shared spaces are conducted frequently and without notice. As such, be sure to keep your quarters clean at all times.

## SCIENCE DECK

*Infinity*'s research laboratories, prototyping workshops, and science staff serve a dual purpose: to store and manufacture experimental technology, and to assess and analyze new phenomenons or alien mechanisms the ship discovers. Because of the nature of their work, the Science Deck contains highly volatile and classified materials, and remains off-limits to most personnel. As a Spartan, you possess a high-level clearance and are allowed limited entry. Remember that many personnel in this section of the ship are civilian contractors, and thus are unaccustomed to military protocol or interacting with Spartans.

## COMMAND BRIDGE

Located at the stern of the vessel, the Command Bridge is where Captain Lasky, Spartan Commander Palmer, and senior staff gather to discuss or implement all broader mission directives and battle plans. The Command Bridge's computer houses slipspace navigational charts, navigational controls for the ship's faster-than-light Shaw-Fujikawa engines, and the core processors for Roland, the ship's AI director. Note that, in the event of the *Infinity* being boarded, the safety and security of the Command Bridge is your highest priority. As the "brain" of *Infinity*, should you lose the Command Bridge, you will lose the ship.

> ### GRANT
>
> There's usually at least two Spartan Fireteams assigned to defend the bridge and Roland's core during a battle, plus the Spartan Mission Directors who stand ready to put on their Mjolnir helmet and pick up an assault rifle.

## PART 02

# THE SPARTAN WAY ///////////

The Spartans of the UNSC take their name from one of human history's most celebrated armed forces. Becoming a modern Spartan is more than simply adopting a moniker; it requires adopting a way of life that mirrors the dedication of our Spartan forebears. The Spartans of the ancient world comprised one of the greatest military forces in history. Hailing from the Greek city-state of Sparta, Spartan children were drafted into the military at the age of seven and raised to be the ultimate warriors. After rigorous training in the art of war, young Spartans were awarded their shields and sent to defend their homeland with their lives.

The young warriors received intensive training in teamwork and weaponry. Spartans lived together, ate together, and were expected to die together. They were trained to fight in a phalanx formation, standing side by side and using their large shields to create a wall to defend against attacking forces. In this formation, they used the dory, a long spear that could strike from behind the shield wall to defend the phalanx, and carried a short sword to fight at close range if the phalanx fell. Most importantly, Spartans were trained to give their all in every battle. These young men were sent to the front lines with one mantra ringing in their heads: Return with your shield, or on it.

We remember these classical Spartans because of one pivotal moment in time, a battle that would save Greece and inscribe the names of these brave warriors into the history books. In 480 BCE, Greece faced annihilation. The overwhelmingly powerful forces of the Persian Empire had invaded the country, and the Greek city-states had no time to evacuate their most vulnerable citizens from threatened regions. In an effort to turn the tide and give the rest of the Greeks time to prepare a counteroffensive, legend says that King Leonidas and 300 of his Spartans waited at the strategic pass of Thermopylae, where they would face King Xerxes and a horde of over 100,000 Persian invaders. Despite being massively outnumbered, the Spartans held the invaders in the pass through two full days of bloody conflict. In the end, they fell, but their sacrifice bought the other Greek city-states valuable time to prepare their defenses against the invaders, and eventually force the Persians from Greek territory at the Battle of Salamis.

This story is an illustration of the duality of Spartan soldiering: what we now call the mastery of the Shield and the Spear. In battle, the classical Spartan hoplites presented an impenetrable front. By locking their shields together into one massive defensive phalanx formation, no force could overcome them. By striking out with their spears, they were able to drive back forces far greater in number and in armament. Yet the shield and spear formation only works so long as each soldier demonstrates a willingness to sacrifice their personal safety and hold the line for the greater good. All Spartan-IV's are expected to display a similar adherence to unit cohesion.

**THE SHIELD AND THE SPEAR** form the basis of Spartan-IV strategy. As the Shield of the UEG, it is your sworn duty to defend civilians from hostile belligerents, alien or domestic, without hesitation. As the UNSC's Spear, your military skill should be employed with absolute precision until the last enemy falls. Make these Spartans proud, recruits.

HUMANITY SALUTES OUR

# *HEROIC SPARTANS*

## WHEN ALL SEEMED LOST IN HUMANITY'S DECADES-LONG WAR WITH THE COVENANT, THE SPARTANS ROSE TO TURN THE TIDES.

MANY UEG CITIZENS HAVE HEARD LEGENDS OF THESE CELEBRATED WARRIORS, BUT WHO ARE THE SPARTANS REALLY? WHERE DID THEY COME FROM? AND WHAT ROLE WILL THEY PLAY IN SECURING HUMANITY'S FUTURE? VISIT YOUR UNSC RECRUITER TODAY FOR AN EXCLUSIVE LOOK AT THE HISTORY OF SPARTANS AND LEARN HOW DISTINGUISHED MILITARY SERVICE CAN BE YOUR STEPPING STONE INTO THE RANKS OF THE LEGENDARY DEFENDERS OF EARTH AND ITS COLONIES!

# UNSC SPARTAN-IV *PROGRAM*

# SUIT UP
## . . . BE A SPARTAN-IV

The Covenant are defeated, but humanity continues to face threats from beyond the stars. Will we embrace our role in the galaxy as the species that defied the Covenant and look to space with hope renewed? Or will we be held back by our fear of the unknown? The future is in YOUR hands. Even as Earth rebuilds and the colonies look to the future, the Spartans stand watch. But the Spartans are few, and the dangers beyond number.

Are YOU prepared to join the most elite combat force ever created and be our first line of defense on the frontier? Veterans of the UNSC Defense Force, Colonial Military Administration, and select Planetary Defense Forces are NOW being accepted for screening to become a member of the most elite military force ever assembled.

ARE YOU ONE OF THOSE PROUD FEW? DO YOU HAVE WHAT IT TAKES? DO YOU WANT TO PROVE YOURSELF? IF SO, NOW IS THE TIME TO SIGN UP, SUIT UP, AND BECOME A SPARTAN.

## UNSC SPARTAN-IV PROGRAM

# SPARTAN-IV

The premise behind the SPARTAN-IV program was simple: use technology developed for the SPARTAN-I and SPARTAN-III programs and meld that with the best qualities of the SPARTAN-II education program. The result would be a new breed of Spartan who could be recruited from the best and brightest UNSC veterans, and then transformed using safe and effective medical procedures to become stronger, faster, and tougher than any normal soldier. New manufacturing methods and scientific advances also made mass-production of Mjolnir armor possible. The combination of new augmentation protocols and next-generation powered assault armor has proven to be a defining capability for the UNSC in the post-war period.

Though there are risks associated with augmenting adults, during the Covenant War the UNSC required a large force of Spartans immediately. Luckily, skilled volunteers inspired by the Master Chief and his fellow Spartans were not in short supply. By recruiting only from the most carefully screened, experienced, and committed warfighters across all UNSC branches, we've expanded our ranks safely, without sacrificing readiness. Trained in all disciplines of war and honed to think strategically, the Spartan-IVs are expert instruments of both war and peace.

Humanity can take comfort in the fact that only the best are selected to wear Mjolnir armor and accepted into our ranks. You, as a Spartan-IV, protect all our hopes for a new generation of pioneers, settlers, and soldiers. For your home and for Earth. For your families and your friends. And for yourself most of all.

Stand tall and proud, for you walk in the company of legends.
We're depending on you.

GRANT

But mostly war.

# SPARTAN-IV
# AUGMENTATIONS

SPARTAN-IV AU

BASELINE PROFILE

CHRL
NRLG
PHNT

⟨✕⟩ TORPET DATACLUSTER INSTALL

As a Spartan-IV, your first challenge will be adapting to a new physical reality. After you awaken from the intensive augmentation surgery, your body will be stronger and faster, and you will find that you can concentrate on tasks and recall facts with ease. Note the following changes, and carefully test your own strength. Newly augmented Spartans have been known to shatter everyday objects with a touch. Use caution until you have completed all rehabilitation protocols.

## 1 – IMPLANTED DATACLUSTER

This neural interface ("'lace'") implant at the base of the skull interacts with your brain and makes you capable of interface with UNSC data systems and any friendly AI's hosted in your Mjolnir armor. You can contact your team members, initiate command protocols, and activate your armor and weapons with a thought.

Neural interface controller

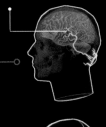

Dataport

## 2 – MUSCULAR AND SKELETAL ENHANCEMENTS

As a Spartan-IV, your bones will be lengthened by several centimeters and strengthened with Titanium-A and composite sheathing. Your muscles will then be reattached and woven with synthetic poly-muscle fibers similar to those used in your exoskeleton suit, which contract with enough force to shatter your original skeleton.

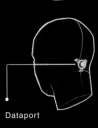

Biomonitoring Implan

⟨✕⟩ MUSCULAR/SKELETAL
ENGINEERING SERIES

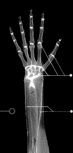

Ligament reconstru
Joint reinforcement

Skeletal fullerene la
Skeletal reenginee

Induced muscle gr
Muscle grafts
completed

TION

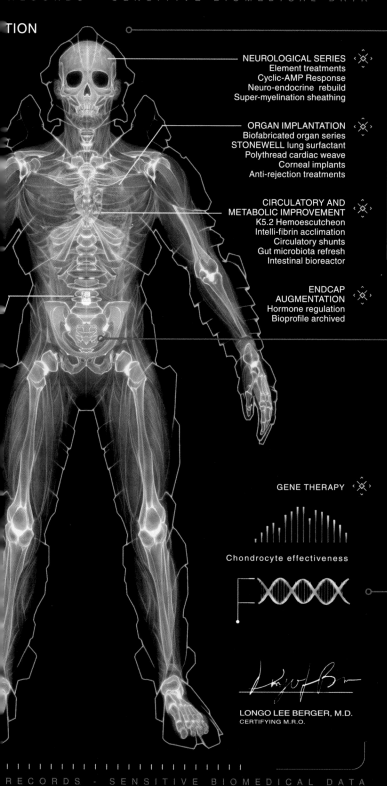

NEUROLOGICAL SERIES
Element treatments
Cyclic-AMP Response
Neuro-endocrine rebuild
Super-myelination sheathing

ORGAN IMPLANTATION
Biofabricated organ series
STONEWELL lung surfactant
Polythread cardiac weave
Corneal implants
Anti-rejection treatments

CIRCULATORY AND
METABOLIC IMPROVEMENT
K5.2 Hemoescutcheon
Intelli-fibrin acclimation
Circulatory shunts
Gut microbiota refresh
Intestinal bioreactor

ENDCAP
AUGMENTATION
Hormone regulation
Bioprofile archived

GENE THERAPY

Chondrocyte effectiveness

LONGO LEE BERGER, M.D.
CERTIFYING M.R.O.

# 3 – NEUROLOGICAL ENHANCEMENTS

These enhancements increase your reaction time in order to give you lightning-fast reflexes and improve your brain's cognitive power. Spartan-IVs exhibit between a 10 to 20 percent improvement in their General Cognitive Propensity (GCP) scores when paired with deep learning methods.

# 4 – PHYSICAL ENHANCEMENT

Cybernetic implants and modified organs make you resistant to toxic environments and chemical attacks. Modified corneas, mechanically aided circulatory systems, and genetically engineered digestive bacteria allow for enhanced night vision, emergency circulatory shunts, and better absorption of nutrients from rations.

# 5 – GENE THERAPY

The full extent of these modifications are classified, but in addition to general health improvements, Spartan augmentation should allow for a longer lifespan. The upper limit of a Spartan-IV's natural lifespan has not been found, but we expect your peak fighting days will exceed a century.

# MJOLNIR POWERED ASSAULT ARMOR

Spartans are hard to kill, but when paired with Mjolnir powered armor they are unstoppable. Developed alongside the Spartan program, Mjolnir armor was created by the legendary skunkworks division of Materials Group, one of the Office of Naval Intelligence's military hardware partners. Created specifically for Spartan physiques, this revolutionary powered assault armor increases your strength, speed, agility, response time, resilience, and overall combat effectiveness in the battlefield. It is designed to be used by biologically augmented personnel only and requires a Spartan neural interface to function. Usage by non-augmented personnel risks serious injury, up to and including limb dislocation and spinal damage. Together, Spartan-IV super-soldier and Generation 2 Mjolnir powered armor constitute a single hyper-lethal combat asset.

## 1 - TECHSUIT

Your Spartan tactical reflex armor is considered part of your uniform, and it is custom-tailored to be comfortable to wear with or without armor attachments. The suit is the polymuscle exoskeleton component of Generation 2 Mjolnir, further increasing your Spartan's agility and raw strength. Note that the suit does not provide physical augmentation without an external power supply. The techsuit is tuned to supplement and complement your specific augmentation profile and provides the arming points on which additional armor components are attached.

## 2 - FRAME

Each Mjolnir class consists of a set of components that are attached to the techsuit's arming points. Most of these are modular armor pieces, though some do incorporate additional electronics and mechanical systems, which augment the user in various ways. The standard set of components and electronic sub-systems is referred to as the frame. A helmet and power pack are added to complete a Mjolnir class set.

## 3 - HELMET

Mjolnir helmets can be used with most frames, but compatibility cannot be assured as the standards and technology evolves. In addition to basic life support and air filtration, the Mjolnir helmet contains a microframe computer core capable of hosting a Smart AI, communications uplink, battle network relay, and sensor systems. All data is compiled and presented to the wearer using a head-up display based on standard UNSC Visual Intelligence System, Reconnaissance (VISR) interfaces.

## 4 - POWER PACK

On most Mjolnir classes, this is a compact fusion reactor, but capacitors and battery systems have also proven useful in specialized applications, such as low-emission stealth operations. In emergencies, the suit's power pack can be tapped much like any other generator, though note that the reactor is not designed for sustained high output. The reactor is located in the rear of suit's armored breastplate and is not Spartan-serviceable.

# MJOLNIR COMPONENTS

## ARMOR PLATES

Inert, but highly resilient plates of metal-matrix composite and Titanium-A add substantial protection against kinetic and plasma weapons, and will erode under directed energy attack, sparing the techsuit and Spartan from damage until they are significantly degraded. While they are relatively simple, Mjolnir armor plate attachments do incorporate waveguides for the energy shield to flow around them, which makes them significantly more expensive than the armor plates used by other UNSC forces. Swapping damaged plates for newly refurbished units upon return to the *Infinity* is standard operating procedure.

## GEL LAYER

The poly-muscle layer in the techsuit replaces the shock-dampening fluid layer from early Mjolnir armor but performs similarly in terms of absorbing the force of heavy impacts and mitigating crushing damage from projectiles. Its active-response functions require power, but even in its inert state the gel layer provides an additional level of ballistic protection.

## LIFE SUPPORT

In addition to air filtration in the helmet, the Mjolnir frame contains a closed-circuit rebreather for operations underwater, in vacuum, and poisonous atmospheres. The system also handles waste processing and recycling during extended field operations.

## MEDICAL SUBSYSTEM

Biofoam injectors and medical gel is automatically dispensed when you are injured. This will stabilize all but the most serious wounds and allow limited combat ability to be retained even in the case of limb loss. The medical subsystem is linked to the battle network and can alert recovery teams in the event of incapacitation.

## ENERGY SHIELDING

When paired with a power pack, the shield generators and distribution webbing in the Mjolnir frame are activated. Based on Covenant technology, the energy shield absorbs and redirects both kinetic and directed energy attacks, though it will temporarily overload and require a recharge if it takes too much damage over a short period of time. The energy shielding is conformal to the body and is channeled around the Spartan through a series of waveguides built into the frame attachments and techsuit. The shield system can be omitted or deactivated if the tactical situation requires, but Spartans are warned that the base Mjolnir armor is insufficient for sustained firefights.

## MOBILITY ENHANCEMENT

The latest Generation 2 Mjolnir incorporates a set of thrusters, which dramatically increases your movement options in a firefight. With experience, Spartans can sprint dash in any direction, ground pound, shoulder charge, clamber up a vertical structure, tactical slide, and stabilize/hover after jumps.

## SMART SCOPE

The built-in targeting and gun-control software of UNSC and Covenant weapons can be directly accessed and controlled by the Mjolnir suit either through contact points built into your techsuit gloves or via wireless data links. In practical terms this means that predicted weapon impact points are always shown in your HUD, or head-up display, as well as diagnostic information about your weapon, such as thermal stress and ammunition count.

## ARTIFICIAL INTELLIGENCES ////////////////

Your Mjolnir armor BIOS is itself a collection of expert systems and non-volitional software packages, but the suit can also host a full Smart AI construct, including its core personality and all attending holographic processing matrices. This creates a technological symbiosis, with the AI having direct access to armor functions and the ability to synchronize with your neural interface. While the AI can increase your reaction time through micromanagement of the suit-Spartan interface layer, the primary purpose of an AI installation is to provide real-time intel analysis and cyberintrusion capabilities. The tactical/strategic coordination of a Smart AI and Spartan is a massive force multiplier, though please be aware that AIs built and trained for this activity are extremely rare and valuable.

### THORNE

If you are selected to partner with a Smart AI, be aware that they are fully independent and self-aware personalities, and by UNSC regulations are to be treated as you would any flesh-and-blood member of your Spartan team.

## BATTLE NETWORK UPLINK /////////

UNSC air, ground, and space forces are all coordinated with a sophisticated communication and decision-support system that allows commanders and boots-on-the-ground warfighters to coordinate their activities and instantly share tactical information. It is through this tactical information management system that UNSC troops pull information from headquarters regarding the position, orientation, and status of enemy combatants, while simultaneously updating friendly units with their own location and activities. These tools greatly simplify the task of troops in clarifying their objectives and allow leaders to manage many combat troops with minimal extra work.

# FIRST DEPLOYMENT

After your augmentation and training cycle, you will be assigned to a Spartan Fireteam and issued your first suit of synchronized Mjolnir powered assault armor. Your Fireteam Leader is responsible for ensuring you follow all rules of engagement and safety protocols, which can vary from each deployment and campaign.

## FIRETEAM ASSIGNMENT

Upon earning the title of "Spartan" you will be assigned to your first field-ready Fireteam. Like the clenched fingers of a mailed fist, up to five Spartan warriors combine their talents to destroy any threat that arises in a hostile galaxy. Spartans are individually powerful—working together they are unstoppable. You'll find that each Fireteam has its own personality, skill set, and unique camaraderie, all of which are integral to completing objectives in the field. During your career you will be a part of many Fireteams, but it is your first assignment that will be the truest test of will and skill.

## EQUIPMENT ISSUE

Aptly named, your initial RECRUIT-class powered assault armor is configured to help you master your new abilities and acclimate to the strain and stress of high-intensity combat operations across diverse battlefields. Once that happens, you will be authorized to select from a range of specialized Mjolnir suit models that complement your combat talents and fieldcraft. You will also be issued both an MA5D Assault Rifle and M6H Magnum as your primary and secondary weapon, respectively. Contact your Fireteam Leader and the *Infinity* armorer to request alternate loadouts.

## ARMOR MOUNTING

Mjolnir armor is extraordinarily heavy and costly, and therefore requires skilled technicians or an automated system to remove the armor piece by piece. In early versions of the armor, technicians would manually encase the Spartan using a variety of mobile systems that could lift and manipulate individual pieces deftly. The *Infinity* uses the latest Brokkr-class multi-axis assembly system to assist Spartans in donning and removing their armor.

## MISSION HANDLER

Your Spartan Fireteam will be assigned a Mission Handler before each operation. This Spartan works directly with the joint planning team aboard the UNSC *Infinity*, ensuring that your activities are fully coordinated with all military forces. Your handler can also provide intelligence analysis and status updates, though you are asked to direct most questions and requests through your Fireteam Leader to avoid possible confusion and duplication of effort.

# TACTICAL ROLE

Every Spartan is a veteran warfighter, and you are trained to be omni-capable on any battlefield. However, Spartans are also expected to bring their unique talents to the fight, and with your Fireteam Leader's permission you may wish to refine and hone your natural abilities even further. No Spartan should over-specialize, but you can find yourself concentrating on improving a broad category of skills that benefit your team in a variety of tactical situations. For convenience, some typical skill groupings are noted below.

## DEFENSIVE

Providing cover for your Fireteam and being a bulwark in intense firefights is appealing to many Spartans. Spartans in this role are given additional training in the art of combat engineering and the use of special equipment, such as portable shield generators, Forerunner constructor beams, and structural hard light emitters. These Spartans excel in holding down the fort and preventing the enemy from pushing on the Fireteam's position.

## DISRUPTIVE

Spartans who have a talent for striking from ambush, hacking, using traps, and general electronic warfare often find themselves drawn to this role. For Spartans, this can mean additional training in the use of optical-cloaking technologies such as active camouflage, qualification with sensor jammers and holographic decoys, and deploying unmanned drones to strike enemies when they least expect it. These Spartans excel in situations where they confound and confuse the enemy, breaking their morale or preventing their special technology from affecting the battle.

## OFFENSIVE

Not every Spartan needs to be subtle. Pure firepower can solve even the thorniest tactical question, and Spartans who serve as agile flankers or direct-action breachers are highly valued by their Fireteam. Spartans in this role practice with heavy weapons and support systems which enable them to push and control, including prototype overshield capacitors and "overclock" software modules. Offensive Spartans excel in taking the fight to the enemy and laying down suppressive fire so their Fireteam can take the initiative.

## SUPPORTIVE

Providing technical support for your Fireteam when on the move is often a critical factor in mission success. Regeneration fields, medical gel dispensers, and extra energy cells are precisely the sort of thing that Spartans need, and you can provide. Spartans in this role excel in keeping the Fireteam in the fight against all odds.

# SPARTAN COMMAND
# STRUCTURE //////////////

Since the creation of the Spartan branch in 2553, we have worked to take the informal leadership traditions of those who wore the Mjolnir before and adapt them into a structure that emphasizes independence and unity of purpose over rigid adherence to chain of command. Nevertheless, you will be given additional responsibilities and authority as you advance in your Spartan-IV career. You will also find yourself in situations in which it is necessary to determine seniority or position in the chain of command relative to other UNSC officers.

# SPARTAN AUTHORITY ///////////////

All Spartans receive a direct commission as an officer in the UNSC. Be aware that a Spartan's authority does not typically extend outside of his or her chain of command. However, UNSC personnel will defer to your expertise in most combat situations and you are expected to take the initiative in any emergency. Spartans follow when necessary but always lead from the front.

| ROLE | RESPONSIBILITIES | UNSC AUTHORITY |
|------|------------------|----------------|
| SPARTAN | AUGMENTED SPECIAL FORCES OPERATIVE EQUIPPED WITH MJOLNIR POWERED ASSAULT ARMOR. | FIRST LIEUTENANT |
| FIRETEAM LEADER | FIELD LEADER FOR A FIRETEAM OF 4–5 SPARTANS. | CAPTAIN |
| MISSION HANDLER | SPARTAN COMMAND LIAISON AND INTELLIGENCE SUPPORT STATIONED AT HEADQUARTERS. RESPONSIBLE FOR MANAGING 5–10 FIRETEAMS; 20–50 SPARTANS. | MAJOR |
| SPARTAN COMMANDER | OVERALL COMMAND-AND-CONTROL OF SPARTAN COMPANY. RESPONSIBLE FOR UPWARDS OF 300 SPARTANS. | COLONEL |
| DIRECTOR OF SPARTAN OPERATIONS | COMMANDER-IN-CHIEF OF THE SPARTANS (CINCSPAR). | GENERAL |

# SPARTAN OPERATIONS

The Spartan branch retains administrative control over all Spartans in the field, but assigning tactical deployments is the responsibility of the Central Command (CentCom) Region in which you are assigned. CentCom is responsible for the allocation of Spartans to the fleets and armies under its control, based on overall strategy and urgent need, and these taskings determine your mission area and chain of command. As a member of the wider UNSC Special Forces community you will work directly with both UNICOM's Special Warfare Command (SpecWar) and NavyCom's Naval Special Warfare Command (NavySpecWar) during deployments. This cooperation allows Spartans to be efficiently deployed to priority tasks on an as-needed basis, so that you can best assist the overall mission of the UNSC.

# PART 03

# PHYSICAL FITNESS GUIDELINES

Spartan augmentation is not just a process that makes you stronger and faster. It's a complete reorientation of the boundaries and basic capabilities of the human physique. You no longer sleep, eat, or think like a normal soldier, and you will not train like one either. Your daily combat simulations, technical briefings, and mental challenges are more than mere workouts, they are vital elements in ensuring that your Spartan body remains in balance and your skills are kept sharp. The tasks set forth in this section will force to the surface your relative strengths and weaknesses as you work with the members of your Fireteam, each of whom will ultimately live or die by your preparedness.

## ANONYMOUS

Spartans are living weapons. And all weapons require precision, maintenance, and skilled use to serve their purpose.

## GRANT

The science is above my paygrade, but Spartan-IV augmentation lacks the stability of earlier generations. While it means that adults can be augmented, it also means we need constant "tune-ups" to ensure that nothing goes out of whack in our bodies.

# AUGMENTATION MONITORING

The biological, chemical, and mechanical enhancements that make up the Spartan augmentation package are tailored specifically for your genetic profile and neurological map. Every Spartan is unique, and there is significant variation in how well you will adapt to the changes or synchronize with particular enhancement profiles. Consult the *Infinity*'s medical support team for the particulars of your individualized maintenance plan.

# SAFETY CONSIDERATIONS

While the full potential of your enhanced physical capabilities are difficult to predict, this is not to say that Spartans should go looking for their limit. Follow all Spartan training guidelines and medical protocols. You are too valuable to endanger just to test the limits of augmentation. In the absence of established benchmarks, we encourage you to find your limits through safely monitored strength training. In the field, Spartans have been recorded lifting Warthogs, bending steel, and shattering concrete. Performing and improving on these feats of strength should serve as inspiration for your training.

Training Note: The War Games training facility is built on a series of hydraulic platforms that lift and move sections of the environment. These platforms can push and pull with tremendous force, and they make for terrific "weight machines" for Spartan-IVs. In your free time, you are encouraged to test your new musculature and bone density in this way with a fellow Spartan.

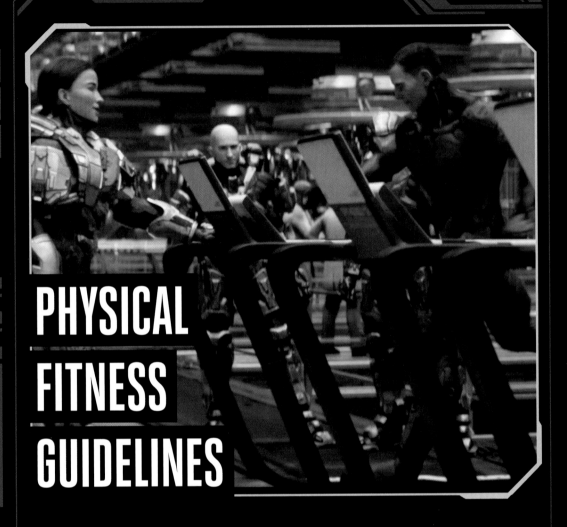

# PHYSICAL FITNESS GUIDELINES

## ENHANCED STAMINA

While Spartan-IVs' neurological and genetic enhancements may turn already exceptionally smart soldiers into expert military minds, there is one critical area that all Spartans should carefully consider before deployment: stamina.

The change most Spartans comment on after waking from augmentation is a reduced need for sleep. You may only feel the need to rest for two hours a day (a feeling that comes more from routine than anything else), but you are not immune to exhaustion. Being a Spartan may require days in active combat or survival scenarios, so it is important to attempt to conserve energy in case you ever find yourself operating in a hostile environment for weeks on end.

# FEATS OF STRENGTH

Spartan-IVs can succeed in virtually any alien battlefield they land on. But making the most of your environment will require an exacting amount of practice with your **athletic** capabilities, both unaided and while wearing Mjolnir powered assault armor.

In most environments, Spartans can achieve running long jumps of several meters and maintain a running speed of 40 km/h (24.9 mph) without Mjolnir armor. And even in standard-to-heavy conventional war gear, your ability to leap, dive, and scale uneven ground surpass the average soldier by a factor of ten or more.

Your augmentations also allow you to consume food that is otherwise indigestible to humans, and your tolerance for temperatures and different atmospheric mixes is increased. With proper acclimation, you can significantly raise the life support duration of your Mjolnir armor, increasing your probability of survival in even the most barren environments.

# VACUUM EXPOSURE

In addition to the abilities listed above, Spartan-IVs have the ability to spacewalk. In a survival situation arising from a ship hull breach or emergency evacuation, you can survive for up to five minutes in the vacuum of space without any equipment, and with minimal mental and physical repercussions. Surviving vacuum exposure can be harrowing for the average human, but your Spartan augmentations make it merely uncomfortable. Be aware that your augmentations provide only limited protection against hard radiation and other hazards often encountered in emergency space walks.

The most dangerous aspect of performing your duties in space is overconfidence. It's easy to overestimate your endurance and resilience to other environmental hazards without the protection of Mjolnir armor, and extreme care should be taken when maneuvering in microgravity to avoid injury or losing control. Do not conduct unprotected space walks except in emergencies or in monitored training environments.

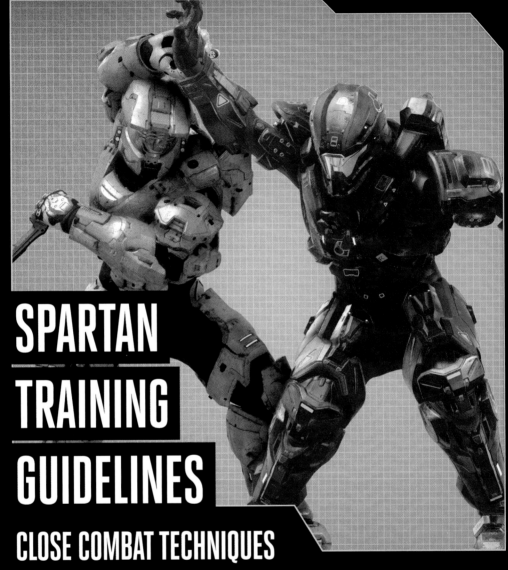

# SPARTAN TRAINING GUIDELINES

## CLOSE COMBAT TECHNIQUES

Every Spartan-IV candidate has basic training in hand-to-hand combat from their previous years of military service, but Spartans are required to learn several fighting styles, as different methods work for different situations. This can mean redirecting the force of a massive Brute's punch with Aikido, disarming an Insurrectionist rebel with Jiu-Jitsu, or taking down a Covenant Elite in close quarters with Krav Maga. Though this may sound daunting, your augmentation gives you the ability to learn new fighting techniques from your opponents—effectively acting as an enhanced "muscle memory" that makes observing and memorizing techniques much easier. To this end, you will be paired with a Spartan who has already mastered the techniques you must learn.

# TRAINING RESPONSIBILITY //////////////

Please note that it is *highly* inadvisable for you to attempt hand-to-hand combat training with any soldier that is not a fellow Spartan. Even in light sparring sessions with non-augmented soldiers, you run a high risk of causing permanent, irreparable harm to them. Furthermore, such a fight would be limited in training value, as your augmentations already make you significantly larger, stronger, and faster than a non-Spartan opponent.

### GRANT

They're not fooling. I heard that some early Spartans had to learn this the hard way.

# SPARTAN TRAINING GUIDELINES

## WEAPONS TRAINING

Like the shields and spears of the Spartan hoplites who came before us, our military weaponry serves a deceptively simple purpose: to create distance between you and your opponents to maximize damage to the enemy and lessen your own risk of harm.

The Spartan-IV armory (see page 176) contains a wide array of modern weaponry. This includes, but is not limited to, close-combat blades, precision firearms, directed energy weapons, missile launchers, and explosives that range from demolition charges to nuclear warheads. You will also be expected to learn the complicated handling and usage instructions for Covenant plasma weaponry, Forerunner hard light projectors, and Brute spike launchers. It is your duty to master all instruments of destruction.

Though you are expected to find a combination of weapons that fit your role in the Fireteam and your natural talents, in combat situations you will be called upon to expertly wield any and every weapon on hand to save a life or complete a mission. Above all else, the most important weapon in your arsenal is your mind; with enough ingenuity, a Spartan can turn any item on hand into a weapon. In all other instances, a Spartan must know the tools of the trade.

## GRANT

I learned a hundred ways to use sharp sticks as a deadly weapon.

## THORNE

If I knew then what I know now, the Covenant wouldn't have had a chance during the war.

# SPARTAN TRAINING GUIDELINES

## COVENANT WEAPONS TRAINING

One of the unique privileges of Spartan training is the opportunity to work with alien weaponry and reverse-engineered prototypes. In the years since the Covenant War ended, we've learned much about the ways that the Covenant's plasma-based systems work, but this technology is still highly volatile and extremely dangerous. During your training, it is recommended that exercises with Covenant tech begin with a review of emergency treatment procedures for plasma burns and handling weapons not designed for human hands. Particular care should be taken when training with the Energy Sword, due to the risk of accidental dismemberment.

# FORERUNNER WEAPONS TRAINING

The exotic hard light weapons used by many Forerunner constructs cannot be replicated by human or Covenant technology, but your Mjolnir armor does have the necessary Smart Scope protocols and decryption matrixes needed to unlock and interface with most examples you acquire on the battlefield. These weapons often feature additional fire modes and alternate functionalities that are not immediately apparent, and you should familiarize yourself with their capabilities in War Games as soon as possible.

### GRANT

Be sure to ask Thorne about his luck in "testing" Forerunner equipment. He's the ship's training dummy when it comes to meddling with new artifacts.

### GRANT

I've watched the techs rip apart those new Banished-manufactured gravitic-catapult spike weapons. They're still scratching their heads trying to figure out how they've made so many improvements, in so short a time.

# BRUTE WEAPONS TRAINING

The spike weaponry and modified Covenant plasma rifles used by the Jiralhanae appear crude, but are highly sophisticated and remarkably lethal. The effectiveness of these weapons should never be underestimated, and ONI has recommended that all Spartan-IVs become qualified in their use to assist in the development of new countermeasures and tactical responses. Additional safety protocols must be followed when training with Brute weaponry, as they lack safety features and are often fitted with unstable power supplies.

# WAR GAMES ///////////////

The primary staging ground for a Spartan's combat training are War Games simulations. Objectives within the War Games training deck are set by Spartan Fireteam Leaders and training specialists on-site. On the UNSC *Infinity*, additional War Games customization capabilities and protocols are available, and these are made available on an as-needed basis by Spartan Commander Palmer.

War Games exercises pit teams of Spartans against each other in an ever-changing arena for physical conditioning, environmental acclimation, weapon familiarization, mission pre-planning, and basic instruction. War Games facilities have several safety protocols and force limiters disabled when being used by Spartan personnel. This increases the value of training in these environments but also increases the chance for injury and equipment damage. No training is without risk, but be aware that the on-duty training supervisor always has final approval over custom scenarios. Use caution during all training exercises.

## THE ARENA

Like the gladiators of old, Spartan teams go head-to-head in the transformable play area of the War Games training deck. The boundaries of the War Games environment are heavily armored and reinforced to withstand a great deal of punishment.

## AUGMENTED REALITY OVERLAY

War Games arena software interfaces directly with your Mjolnir's feedback systems and heads-up display to simulate imaginary locations or re-create any recorded environment down to individual blades of grass. The *Infinity* has first-tier systems and map designers, with arena programs that connect to Spartan neural interfaces to make the simulation even more realistic.

## MODULAR ENVIRONMENTS

Without the virtual- and augmented-reality overlays to mask their appearance, War Games environments are complicated arrangements of transforming obstacles and markers that can be configured to mimic the layout and shape of buildings, enemy vessels, rocks, fusion reactors, and countless other places to hide for a sneak attack or traverse to flank an enemy.

## WEAPONS AND OBJECTIVES

Weapons and power-ups can be placed in a War Games environment as play aids and for training. Competitive matches that pit Spartans against each other in these friendly games of skill build Fireteam cohesion and push you toward ultimate readiness in any situation imaginable.

## MUNERA PLATFORMS:

The *Infinity* has an extensive War Games facility, but most ships are not sizeable enough to hold large exercises. At most naval depots and training facilities, War Games environments are built into specialized Munera Platforms. These training facilities create the perfect environments in which to display martial skill, test the latest military technology, and broadcast competitive Spartan exercises to audiences around the UEG to build morale.

### GRANT

I believe the public relations folks call it "forging a positive narrative."

## ANVIL INITIATIVE:

The Anvil Initiative is a cross-training and evaluation program operated in collaboration with our Sangheili allies, the Swords of Sanghelios. Anvil provides Spartans the opportunity to directly interact and train with their Elite counterparts in both shared War Games and live exercises. This unique evaluation program also tests the latest hybrid technologies developed by ONI, UNSC corporate partners, Sangheili artisan-armorers, and special research collaborations. The location of the Anvil Initiative and the details of participation are classified, and access is by invitation only.

### THORNE

An opportunity to train with Sangheili swordmasters? Sign me up.

### GRANT

An opportunity to watch Thorne get schooled by Elites? Sign me up as well.

### THORNE

Laugh it up, I've ran the simulations. I'm at least at neophyte rank now. How about it, newbie, want to spar next time we're in War Games?

# PART 04

# A HISTORY OF //////////
# THE SPARTAN PROGRAM

By joining the SPARTAN-IV program, you are continuing a long tradition of excellence in service. Spartans played an instrumental role in ending the Covenant War and setting the stage for the next great era of human civilization. As a member of this storied organization, you are expected to understand the role Spartans have played in the past, and what will be expected of you in the future.

Every child born in the modern age—whether in the Sol system or in the farthest reaches of our many colonial outposts—knows the official history of the Covenant War. That bloody struggle saw countless planets reduced to glass by an alien empire of seemingly unstoppable might. The Covenant could not be negotiated with or threatened, and they refused all attempts at diplomacy. While we won some hard-fought victories, their technological superiority and limitless numbers pushed the UNSC to its limits. Only exceptional heroism and tireless patriotism delivered us a victory in our darkest hour.

But what few have been allowed to know until now is the true history of how Spartan efforts allowed humanity to triumph. Even as they fought battle after battle to turn Covenant forces away, Spartan soldiers had to work in secret; even as they sacrificed themselves to hold back the Covenant tide from engulfing more worlds, the stories of their courage and dedication had to remain highly classified. If their true role had been publicized during the war, the Covenant might have found a way to counter our Spartans' valorous efforts, removing our one key advantage over the Covenant war machine.

The next chapter of the Spartan story will be written by YOU, the next generation of Spartan-IVs. As new threats arise, you are needed more than ever. You are no longer in the shadows of history, you are writing it.

This is their story. This is your legacy.

### THORNE

Now this is more my speed! Even if we all know this is a "creative" interpretation of events.

### GRANT

The official records gloss over a lot of things, but everyone does their best to forget just how devastating the Covenant War was. And how close we came to extinction.

### THORNE

The Spartans can't afford to forget what's at stake.

# COLONIZATION

As we all know, in 2291, the creation of the Shaw-Fujikawa Translight Engine (SFTE) opened up the stars to human exploration and colonization. With the SFTE, the strange multi-dimensional realm known as slipspace could be used to travel many light-years in a matter of months, rather than centuries. Billions left the familiar light of Sol for distant stars, though these journeys were often perilous and long. Colonies were established in dozens of star systems, some on planets that proved capable of supporting human life without sealed habitats and extensive terraforming. New terraforming technologies were introduced at a rapid pace, allowing marginal worlds to be altered in the span of mere decades and slipspace drives became safer and cheaper.

# INSURRECTION

But the colonies remained a harsh environment for survival and expansion for many decades, particularly as communication was slow and unreliable, with messages sometimes taking years to cross between colonies separated by lengthy slipspace routes. Even with these challenges, by 2400 we had created unimaginable beauty on dozens of worlds and in thousands of orbital habitats. From the picturesque grain fields of Harvest to the orbital shipyards of Neos Atlantis, mankind was quickly making its mark on the galaxy. But even as mankind spread, the seeds of rebellion and terrorism began to appear as malcontents and criminals gathered at the fringes of civilization. It was soon apparent that a radical solution was necessary to contain this growing threat to the peace and prosperity in the colonies.

The Insurrection was—and remains—the UEG's greatest internal security challenge. Combating the rebels required the might of the entire UNSC, and this struggle was central to the foundation of the Spartans. In an attempt to bring peace to the colonies, the Spartan super-soldier programs sought to deliver an army of brave men and women with the ability to defend the citizens of humanity against all threats.

# PROJECT: ORION

The first steps toward the development of Spartan super-soldiers dates to before the era of interstellar exploration, when five brave volunteers were accepted into the first Project: ORION on April 13, 2321. While this original program is generally considered to have failed in delivering a new breed of super-soldier—the cost of augmentation and the risks that volunteers faced made its large-scale implementation unfeasible—the advances its scientists made in bionic implantation and gene therapies were revolutionary.

Although the project was never widely implemented, we now consider the participants in Project: ORION the first true generation of Spartans. While their time was brief, their success in countering terrorist and criminal activity in the colonies was a crucial factor in the approval of future super-soldier initiatives.

# SPARTAN-II

By the early 26th century, criminality and chaos in the colonies forced a radical response. In 2517, using Project: ORION as a template, ONI set out to create a new ultra-tech police and counterterrorism force, which would eliminate these disruptive elements of interstellar society and return order to the UEG. This would become the fabled Project: SPARTAN-II. The best and brightest of humanity were recruited and brought together to create the next generation of super-soldier.

Unlike its forbearer, SPARTAN-II imagined a breed of soldier and civil servant unlike any in human history. These Spartans wouldn't simply be stronger soldiers. They would be skilled diplomats and peerless strategists who could forge peace when strength of arms was insufficient. This new breed of warrior-scholars were recruited at a young age to enter an elite military academy and given the most intensive physical and intellectual training that technology allowed. Amid the mountains of Reach, seventy-five young volunteers were accepted from the best humanity had to offer, and came of age with the defense and protection of human civilization as their sole mission.

## THORNE

This is completely bogus. The records are still locked, but it's clear the Spartan-IIs were never "volunteers."

# THE SPARTAN-II REVOLUTION

Credit for the SPARTAN-II program is shared by many brilliant icons in the UEG. Skilled instructors, dedicated scientists, and motivated engineers combined their efforts to shape young recruits and mold them into Spartans, and in the process built a new idea of what service to humanity looked like. When we speak of duty, honor, and sacrifice in our own Spartan training, we look to this first class of heroes for inspiration and guidance.

As the first class of Spartan-II initiates began their training on Reach, their trainers and teachers sharpened minds and bodies to a keen edge. Working in teams that developed over years at the academy, young Spartans were able to outwit and outfight even experienced soldiers in countless training scenarios and military exercises. By the time the Spartan-IIs were ready for their final augmentation, they were already an elite fighting force.

# THE MASTER CHIEF ///////////////

One Spartan-II recruit in particular stood out among this group of prodigies: a young scrapper and troublemaker from Eridanus II. His full name remains classified at the highest levels to protect those close to him, but his fellow Spartan-IIs knew him by the call sign John-117. Uncommonly skilled and courageous, John-117 quickly rose through the Navy special forces community to the rank of Master Chief, developing his skills as a leader and warfighter over the course of the Covenant War.

What made John-117 such an outstanding Spartan remains hard to define. It could have been his competitive streak or his unflagging loyalty, or maybe what set him apart was his empathy and sense of duty—the way he fought hard in every no-win situation to preserve human life above his own. Or, more likely, it was the way the Master Chief combined these qualities to show us all what a hero is supposed to be. Whatever alchemy created him, John-117 was unanimously selected by his peers as the leader of the Spartan-IIs. When he strapped on the then-experimental Mjolnir powered assault armor, he became the hero who would save humanity and usher in a golden age of peace and prosperity.

# THE COVENANT WAR

On February 11, 2525, humanity made first contact with the alien alliance known as the Covenant on the remote colony world of Harvest. Within two weeks, the majority of Harvest was utterly destroyed by the Covenant's advanced weaponry. With that opening salvo, a nearly thirty-year war for survival began. It can only now be acknowledged how completely the Covenant put humanity on its heels in those early days of the war and drove us to the very brink of extinction.

Today we have learned much about why the Covenant attacked our worlds and burned our cities. Experts posit that the mere existence of humans upset the prophecies that had kept the Covenant's religious leaders in power for thousands of years. But we had no way of knowing their motivation in those early years, nor could we comprehend the enormous technological advantage they had in weaponry, armor, and slipspace drives. In fact, the UNSC couldn't even confirm the loss of Harvest for months after it happened, as couriers and messengers slowly made their way back to UNSC headquarters on Reach and Earth.

But even when our fate seemed hopeless, the Spartans held firm.

# SPARTANS ENTER THE WAR

The newly minted Spartan-IIs found both their calling and their baptism by fire in that initial decade of the Covenant War. Early in the conflict, the first class of super-soldiers were broken into smaller combat teams and deployed to critical war zones, taking the fight to the Covenant in any way they could.

The odds seemed stacked against the UNSC and our Spartans at every turn. With their massive carriers and planet-burning plasma weaponry, the Covenant invaded with millions of fanatical warriors who destroyed everything in their path. Opposing such a force, a small band of Spartan super-soldiers may have seemed less than adequate. The key to Spartan-II victories during the Covenant War was the units' surgical precision and adherence to secrecy. Virtually unknown to the majority of the UNSC, and appearing to the enemy only as ghostly demons who could somehow best even the Covenant's Elite warriors, Spartans proved incredibly effective at securing intelligence from behind enemy lines while also keeping secrets like the true location of Earth out of Covenant hands.

During these early conflicts, the Master Chief cemented his legendary status. John-117's Blue Team fought on dozens of besieged worlds, buying valuable time for orderly UNSC withdrawals and civilian evacuations, and leading strikes deep into the heart of the enemy forces to destroy key ships and eliminate Covenant commanders. Due to their extraordinary successes in the face of overwhelming odds, the Spartan-IIs and the Master Chief are rated as "hyper-lethal" by ONI tactical analysts.

# SPARTAN-III

As the Spartan-IIs held the line during the darkest days of the Covenant War, ONI moved forward with the next phase of the Spartan program in hopes that its successes could be duplicated and even amplified on a massive scale. Using the latest technology and experience gained from augmenting the Spartan-IIs, the UNSC initiated a bold plan to train and equip entire companies of super-soldiers. And thus, the Spartan-IIIs were born.

Spartan-IIIs were unique in many respects. The augmentation process that took them from young recruit to fully fledged super-soldier was streamlined, and their training focused entirely on the skills needed to take the fight to the Covenant. Though they lacked the all-round knowledge of their predecessors, the Spartan-IIIs were almost their equal in a firefight. Unfortunately, the Mjolnir armor could not be manufactured at the scale needed to equip every new super-soldier. The lighter, stealthier Semi-Powered Infiltration (SPI) armor systems they were issued couldn't match Mjolnir in full, but it could be mass-produced and provided excellent protection against Covenant weaponry.

Tragically, despite their technical and physical enhancements, few Spartan-IIIs lived to see the end of the war. The Spartan-IIIs were sent on the most audacious and dangerous operations of the entire war, deploying deep behind enemy lines to attack staging areas and strategic targets protected by entire legions of Covenant forces. These missions delayed the Covenant war machine for months, at the cost of hundreds of brave Spartan-III lives. Their sacrifice will never be forgotten.

# THE FALL OF REACH

Fresh from a victory at Sigma Octanus IV and several other successful operations against the Covenant, hopes were high in late 2552 that the Covenant advance was faltering, and a daring mission to force a ceasefire with the alien leadership was planned. The remaining Spartan-IIs were assembled for this mission, codenamed Operation: RED FLAG, while the Spartan-IIIs continued to strike at Covenant bases to delay and distract their armies and fleets. But even as the UNSC prepared this counteroffensive, the Covenant marshalled its strength and struck at the very heart of the UEGs defenses: the fortified colony of Reach. Heavily guarded by defense platforms in orbit and garrison troops on the ground, the planet was the cornerstone of humanity's military might.

The Covenant armada, which attacked Reach on August 30, 2552, was the largest ever seen. The defenders of Reach were valiant, inflicting massive damage to the attacking Covenant fleet and its legions. The Spartans were invaluable in this defensive campaign, fighting almost to the last, despite being outnumbered a thousand to one. Not many would survive the fall of Reach. Countless Spartans, naval officers, soldiers, and innocent citizens were killed when the Covenant finally struck with its full strength, but their deaths would not be in vain. Even in the face of absolute destruction, these brave defenders bought time for Earth to prepare its own defenses and plan for the final assault.

When the doom of Reach appeared inevitable, Operation: RED FLAG was initiated. Master Chief boarded the UNSC *Pillar of Autumn* to make a daring strike against the Covenant, following intelligence gathered from Covenant forces on Sigma Octanus IV, they initiated a slipspace jump to a mysterious set of coordinates. By chance, they arrived not at a Covenant capital, but near what we now know as Alpha Halo, or Installation 04.

# DISCOVERY OF THE HALO RINGS

On September 19, 2552, the UNSC *Pillar of Autumn* emerged from slipspace in a star system on the edge of known space. Before them was an artificial ringworld 10,000 kilometers (6,213 miles) in diameter, surrounded by a Covenant fleet, which had followed the humans from Reach. The discovery of the Halo ring sent shockwaves through the Covenant leadership and triggered the beginning of both a religious and political crisis, though this was not apparent to the UNSC at the time.

Master Chief's orders were clear: Protect the *Pillar of Autumn* and secure any data that could potentially lead the Covenant to Earth. The legendary Spartan led the defense of the ship against waves of Covenant boarding parties, until critical damage forced the captain to order a full evacuation onto the nearby ring. Saving as many crew as he could, the Master Chief was the last aboard the *Autumn*'s escape pods.

# THE ALPHA HALO CONFLICT

The surface of the Halo was a terraformed environment that simulated the environment of a planet in almost every detail. Though it was devoid of any sapient life, the ring was obviously engineered to hold many kinds of living creatures and plant life. Dotting its carefully sculpted landscapes were massive Forerunner buildings, hinting at the kilometers-deep network of machinery hidden beneath the surface.

On the surface of the ring, UNSC forces quickly seized the initiative over the Covenant, regrouping and preparing for a textbook guerrilla campaign while they searched for some means to control the massive installation. The Master Chief proved himself to be the prime example of a Spartan soldier by fighting through Covenant forces to recover stranded UNSC soldiers, and then lead a daring assault aboard a Covenant carrier to rescue those who had been captured during the evacuation.

The discovery and capture of the ring's key map room revealed the location of the ring's central control room. Despite heavy Covenant opposition and the challenge of operating in such a strange environment, the Master Chief assaulted the control room, single-handedly defeating an entire Covenant cohort in the process.

# ALPHA HALO'S DESTRUCTION

While the Master Chief was tasked with accessing the Halo ring's control room and investigating how the ancient Forerunner technology could potentially be turned to humanity's advantage, a second detachment serving under the command the *Pillar of Autumn*'s Captain Jacob Keyes sought out the weapons cache Covenant troops had located on the ring. Only one of these missions ended in success.

Ultimately, there was no weapons cache hidden in Halo. What the second team encountered—and inadvertently released—was the Flood: an omni-parasitic species that had overwhelmed and nearly defeated the Forerunners in the distant past. Those they infect have their bodies hijacked and memories harvested for the location of new potential victims. As new Spartans, you might eventually face the terrifying power of the Flood. You must understand this enemy so you can avoid the horrible fate of the Flood's early human victims.

At the time, the Covenant and UNSC forces on the ring were unprepared for how quickly the Flood could adapt to attempts at containment and how easily it could infect both human and alien soldiers. The outbreak soon grew out of control, despite the Master Chief's best efforts.

//////////////

Though he was too late to rescue the UNSC officers and soldiers, the Master Chief did make first contact with the Halo ring's caretaker, a Forerunner monitor that called itself 343 Guilty Spark. The monitor presented itself to the Master Chief as the benign administrator of the Halo facility and sent the Spartan on a quest for the Halo's Activation Index—which it claimed was the key to stopping the spread of the Flood. The Master Chief soon deduced that this solution to the Flood would require activating the Halo ring, resulting in disastrous consequences for all life within thousands of light-years around the installation.

//////////////

With typical Spartan ingenuity and expertise, the Master Chief solved the threat of the Flood infestation and simultaneously dealt a blow to the Covenant. In a daring move that only a Spartan could hope to accomplish, he raced against time and set the crippled UNSC *Pillar of Autumn* to self-destruct, destroying the ring, the Flood outbreak, and an entire Covenant fleet. The few UNSC survivors regrouped and made their way back to Earth with invaluable intelligence about the Forerunners, Flood, and the Covenant.

### GRANT

Or, according to ONI records, thanks to Cortana hacking the Halo's data systems to discover its true function.

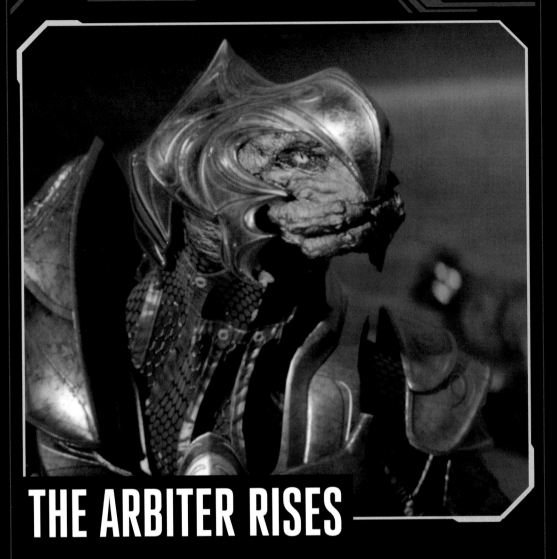

# THE ARBITER RISES

What the rest of us did not realize until much later is that the discovery of Halo created a rift among the Covenant command. Leading the Covenant were the High Prophets, a triumvirate of San'Shyuum clerics who controlled every aspect of their vast realm. Named after the qualities they were supposed to embody, the High Prophets of Truth, Mercy, and Regret had insisted upon the total annihilation of humanity based on their interpretation of Forerunner records regarding our species. We know now that these Covenant rulers believed that the ancient Forerunners had used the Halo rings to transcend the physical world, unaware that these constructs were, in fact, a weapon system designed to destroy all sentient life in order to stop the Flood. As Forerunner records indicated that humanity had a special role in the plans of the ancient species, humans were seen as a threat to the Covenant's Great Journey, a journey that would end in the Prophets becoming gods.

As questions about the Great Journey began to spread among the population, the three Prophets were forced to accelerate their own plots to prevent insurrection. Their first move was to punish the disgraced Sangheili fleet commander from the Alpha Halo, Thel 'Vadamee, for his "heresy" by naming him an Arbiter. Arbiter was a special role originating in ancient Sangheili history reserved for those Elites who sought to recover their honor through extreme acts of self-sacrifice; in Thel 'Vadamee's case, this meant taking on impossible tasks at the behest of the Prophets.

Despite a continued effort to appear united, each Prophet pursued his own plot to take sole control of the Covenant and eliminate any potential rivals that would deny his right to be first among the new gods. The discovery of Alpha Halo had only further proven their beliefs, and the Prophets knew it was only a matter of time before a new Halo was found and their ascension could begin.

# BATTLE FOR EARTH

The Prophet of Regret was the first to act, traveling to what he thought was a hidden Forerunner facility on a planet the Covenant had never reached—Earth—although thankfully he did not realize he'd found the human homeworld. Assuming the humans living on Earth were keeping the Forerunner data he sought hidden for their own heretical ends, the Prophet pressed the attack on the planet before reinforcements could arrive or the other Prophets could discover his plans. Many Spartans in active service lost friends and family to this first attack on Earth, and we all owe a debt to the Master Chief for preventing the loss of even more human life.

On October 20, 2552, the Prophet of Regret's fleet engaged the surprised orbital defense forces of Earth, where the Master Chief, charged with defending Cairo Station, picked up a bomb conveniently left behind by a Covenant boarding party and delivered it into the heart of an attacking Covenant carrier. The Chief's actions resulted in the complete destruction of a Covenant assault carrier, a major victory against the fleet, and an excellent example of what one determined Spartan can do against impossible odds. The Prophet's flagship used the rest of his fleet as a shield, penetrating UNSC defenses and making a forced landing on Earth itself. None of us will ever forget the Battle for Earth that ensued; months of desperate fighting across the planet finally ended in a human victory, though at a terrible cost.

Military scholars will write about the Battle for Earth for generations to come. For our purposes, it cannot be understated how critical it was that the Master Chief himself arrived planetside in pursuit of the Prophet of Regret. With characteristic bravery, the Spartan literally launched himself into the fray at the head of an emergency UNSC task force that moved to engage the Covenant landing forces and aid in the city's evacuation. While the Master Chief could not single-handedly stop the Covenant's legions from recovering the Forerunner data they sought, he did delay the Prophet long enough to allow the UNSC *In Amber Clad* to follow him as he escaped into slipspace.

But it is important to remember that the Master Chief was not solely responsible for winning the Battle for Earth. Battle hardened veterans and new recruits were joined by regular citizens who took up arms to defend their homes. Inspired by the public revelation of the Spartan program, humanity joined together in what most believed was our final hour. Our job as Spartans is to ensure that no disaster like the Battle for Earth can ever happen again.

# THE GREAT SCHISM

On board the UNSC *In Amber Clad*, the Master Chief and Commander Miranda Keyes chased the fleeing Prophet of Regret away from Earth and to a newly discovered Halo installation, where the Chief's legend rose to new heights. On this installation, which the UNSC has designated Delta Halo, the Covenant's leadership finally shattered. Master Chief avenged our colonies and Earth's defenders, eliminating the Prophet of Regret. But the hardest fight was still ahead of him.

The loss of Regret upset the delicate balance of power in the Covenant. Each calling upon his allies, the remaining Prophets moved quickly to consolidate power. Lusting after the power of Halo and the promise of transcendence, the Prophets enacted a plan to take control of the Halo ring. But the growing internal strife within the high orders of the Covenant coincided with an even more dangerous Flood threat that emerged on the newly discovered Halo installation. The infestation spread quickly, inadvertently aided by the jealous interference of the Prophets as they plotted for control of the ring.

In a chamber beneath the structure, the Master Chief and the Arbiter were forced to work together to overcome a Flood infestation. Here, confronted with the true purpose of the Halo Array, the Arbiter suffers a crisis of faith and agreed to work with the Master Chief to stop the spread of the Flood and prevent the activation of the Halo ring. As the Arbiter worked to retrieve the Activation Index, the Chief chased the Prophets of Truth and Mercy to end the Covenant's remaining leadership once and for all. He arrived on the Covenant's capital, High Charity, only to find it heavily infected by the Flood. Leaving Mercy to his fate, the Chief followed Truth aboard an ancient Forerunner dreadnought as he raced toward Earth.

# THE COVENANT
# WAR ENDS

Returning to an Earth still under siege, the Master Chief joined the Arbiter and a group of UNSC personnel and set out to stop Truth from using the Forerunner portal complex to access the Ark and gaining control of the Halo Array. Risking their lives in the effort, the Chief and the Arbiter followed Truth to the Ark and fought both the remnants of the Covenant and the Flood infested High Charity. Together, they managed to use a replacement Halo installation, still under construction in the Ark, to destroy the Flood, shut down the portal, and end Truth, the last remaining High Prophet of the Covenant. While the Arbiter and the remaining UNSC troops escaped, the Master Chief stayed behind to finish the fight.

Though the Master Chief was missing, and Earth had suffered greatly, the High Prophets were dead, their capital ship destroyed, and the Covenant armies on Earth had been decimated by UNSC defenders and by their own civil war. It was clear that the war had come to an end, but the sheer scale of destruction and casualties on both sides were almost impossible to calculate. All of us remember the memorial services honoring the Covenant War's dead, where the Arbiter stood alongside UNSC leadership and signified a new alliance between the Sangheili and humanity.

After the last of the Covenant was routed from the Sol star system and humanity's remaining colonies, the Arbiter and his fleet returned to Sanghelios, eager to destroy the remnants of Truth's forces and free their own people from the Covenant's lies. This critical alliance would have never been possible were it not for the comradery and trust that the Master Chief had built with the Sangheili leader over countless battles, fighting back-to-back on Earth and on the Ark.

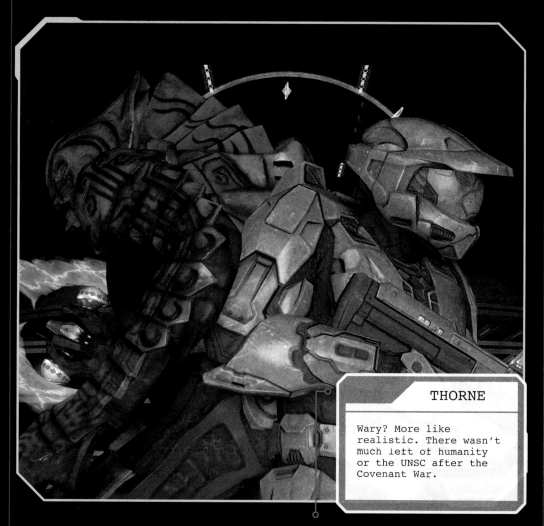

### THORNE

Wary? More like realistic. There wasn't much left of humanity or the UNSC after the Covenant War.

After decades of war and suffering, many were wary of what the future would hold. And so, those of us responsible for the Spartan legacy were given a mandate: Rebuild the Spartans as defenders of humanity, and protect all that those who came before us fought, and died, to achieve. We must study our past to keep our future safe. Remembering the lessons of the Covenant War is essential for those of you who want to become part of the new Spartan vanguard.

# REQUIEM

We now know that when the Ark's portal collapsed, the Master Chief was transported to the Epoloch star system, deep in uncharted space. Placing himself in cryosleep, the Master Chief drifted for six years until he was pulled inside Requiem, a moon-sized Forerunner fortress. Awakened, but stranded, the Master Chief discovered a Covenant group under an Elite called Jul 'Mdama attempting to capture Requiem and use it against his enemies on Earth and Sanghelios.

Though the UNSC's flagship *Infinity* soon arrived to support the Chief, its crew was unable to defeat both the Covenant and the Forerunner constructs they had marshalled to their cause. The *Infinity*'s captain made the difficult decision to return to Earth and bring back reinforcements, but the Master Chief volunteered to stay on Requiem to delay the vicious Covenant attack for as long as possible.

Heedless of the danger and in the face of overwhelming odds, the Master Chief successfully infiltrated the Covenant command ship, engaged the ship's captain in hand-to-hand combat, and successfully destroyed the mighty warship with a nuclear warhead he had smuggled aboard. But no victory comes without sacrifice, and even the Master Chief was unable to prevent the Covenant from making one final strike against Earth before their defeat, killing the innocent civilian population of New Phoenix.

# REQUIEM LOST //////////////////

Inspired by the valiant efforts of the Master Chief, the UNSC deployed the *Infinity* and a support fleet to prevent the Covenant from using Requiem to make any further attacks on Earth. Spartan-IVs led the assault, seizing critical landing zones in the artificial world. The remaining Covenant forces activated Requiem's self-destruct when it became clear that the Spartan-IVs were closing on his position. Leaving many of his troops to die, Jul 'Mdama retreated as Requiem plunged into Epoloch. The Spartan-IVs of the *Infinity* continue to hunt for Jul 'Mdama, and stand ready to strike when the Covenant leader emerges from hiding.

### GRANT

Just a gut feeling, but there's no way that a Forerunner machine the size of a small planet would be destroyed by something as boring as being plunged into a star.

### THORNE

The Forerunners called Requiem a shield world. It was more of a grave world.

# PART 05

# ONI
# AUGMENTATION
# REPORT

# RESTRICTED ONI MESSAGE
## ///EYES ONLY TOP SECRET///

## SHA 001-458 SUMMARY OF HUMAN AUGMENTATION PROGRAMS 2100-2557 CE

SUMMARY: This document is a revision of the ONI Consolidated Weapon Platform Review 2553 (ONITR-09121-ST09-SPT), updated by HighCom for Fleet Admiral Hood, Chairman of the UNSC Security Council.

**MEMORANDUM**
**21 June 2320**

**FROM: Dr. Greenberg, Program Supervisor**
**TO: Colonial Administration Authority, KYKLOS Working Group**

Ladies and gentlemen, I am pleased to announce we have completed our last milestone for Sequence Zero deliverables. Key accomplishments are summarized below.

## NEUROLOGICAL ADJUSTMENTS

Final candidate series has been screened for compatibility with Dr. Shephard's cyclic-AMP response element binding protein (also known as CREB) treatment. Initial results indicate an order of magnitude improvement in information retention and spatial memory formation.

## IDENTITY REGULATION

KYKLOS biosculpting protocols adapted from existing undercover mission packages and refined to defeat facial recognition algorithms and Level-II bioassays that rely on vein patterns. All candidates have completed WHISPERPETAL mode training for personality emulation.

## PERSONALITY FRAGMENTION

Dr. Shephard remains concerned with the personality fragmentation and short-term amnesia exhibited by 70% of subjects during the Sequence Zero destructive testing. Full genetic screening should reduce side effects of the training and treatment regime, but close monitoring of candidates during their first deployment is highly recommended.

# ORION PHASE 1

## DATES ACTIVE:
2315–2325

## PROJECT SPONSOR:
UEG \\ Colonial Military Administration \\ KYKLOS

## PROJECT LEAD:
DR. RITSA SHEPHARD

## BACKGROUND:
An extension of "blue sky" projects commissioned by the UEG before the first interstellar colonization vessel was launched, the ORION research program was focused on applying new developments in biotechnology for military use. Human trials with volunteers began in 2321 and ran until 2325, when the program was officially put on standby and staff reassigned.

## DEPLOYMENT:
Seven volunteers successfully completed prototype ORION bodysculpting, transplant integration, and neurosurgery cycle. Size of initial recruitment pool and long-term health assessments are not available.

## RESULTS:
The first ORION initiative was hampered by poor personnel retention, as key staff joined colonization missions or were transferred to terraforming research. Consistency of the program was also problematic, with significant performance variation between augmentation candidates. While the early ORION work demonstrated potential in exploiting genetic and tissue engineering technology for soldier enhancement, costs were high, and reliability was low. Major aspects of this program remain undocumented, as several encrypted UEG digital archives from this period have degraded or gone missing.

# ORION AUGMENTATION

**REQUEST BY CC-409871 – [ORION PROTOCOL SUMMARY] –
2510:12:08:23:02:15:57**

Ma'am, I've simplified and summarized the information we've been given
regarding the ORION Project and associated protocols. This should be
sufficient for your meeting with the stakeholders while you continue the
onboarding and security clearance process. Unfortunately, your request to
interview and conduct a tissue biopsy series on active-duty ORION personnel
has been rejected.

## REQUEST 1 - GENE THERAPY RESULTS
Records Attached: 459 (2 pending review)
ORION candidates underwent a series of gene-therapy treatments intended
to significantly increase their cognitive and neurological adaptability. Though
results were promising, there were significant side effects. Over half of the
candidates suffered from DNA fragmentation and irreversible damage to
the genetic integrity of their gametes. I've attached the genetic profiles and
timelines for your review.

## REQUEST 2 - SKELETAL REINFORCEMENT PROTOCOLS
Records Attached: 14 (129 pending review)
All IRIS augmentation protocols begin with the installation of a semi-fullerine
lattice around load-bearing bones. Late-series upgrade procedures added
gengineered bone marrow cells, which produce enhanced red and white blood
cells. We are still processing your Special Access Program credentials, but
once that is cleared you will have access to all medical records and research
notes on these procedures.

## REQUEST 3 - STATUS GUARD EXPLOITS
Records Attached: 23 (11 pending review)
Embedded BYZANTINE JARGOON virus in medical records is tailored to
exploit UEG identity confirmation routines and routine medical diagnostics
to guarantee operative anonymity and avoid implant detection. Payload
was tested and confirmed during ORION candidate travel to Seongnam
augmentation site and follow-on mission activations. Your personal AI has
already been upgraded to bypass BYZANTINE restrictions.

# ORION PHASE 2 (SPARTAN-I)

## DATES ACTIVE:
2491–2506

## PROJECT SPONSOR:
UEG \\ UNSC \\ Navy \\ ONI \\ Section Three \\ IRIS

## PROJECT LEAD:
REAR ADMIRAL PRANAV SABANIS

## BACKGROUND:
Administratively an extension of the original ORION to benefit from its continuing authority and ethical waivers, the Office of Naval Intelligence took over management of the inactive project from the CMA in exchange for unspecified concessions. Development timelines indicate that most elements of the new program had been completed before ONI consolidated work under Project: ORION.

## DEPLOYMENT:
Three hundred candidates were selected for ORION augmentation between 2491 and 2505. One hundred and sixty-five ORION assets are recorded as being active when the program was shut down in 2506. Augmentation success appears exceptional, though most ORION assets experienced shortened lifespans during the Covenant War. Strategic results from Operation: CHARLEMAGNE and KALEIDOSCOPE were very promising, but resource limitations and reorganization of the CMA resulted in project closure. Project: ORION was officially redesignated as SPARTAN-I in 2513, after ONI absorbed all project assets for its own super-soldier program.

## RESULTS:
Information on augmentation and training failures is currently unavailable, though evidence suggests high success rate of biochemical modifications, neurological implants, and skeletal grafts. Failure rates with cardiovascular enhancements and cybernetic reinforcement were far higher, with reversion needed in several cases. Genetic therapy proved unreliable on adult candidates, leading to cancers and degenerative neurological conditions in several subjects.

# SPARTAN-II AUGMENTATION

## OPERATION: TALON

Operation: TALON (September 12-14, 2525) was the first real-world mission executed by SPARTAN-II candidates. Blue Team was deployed against the rebel threat they had trained to fight for nearly a decade. TALON was explicitly created to root out the Insurrection leader Colonel Robert Watts from a hidden base located in an asteroid belt near Eridanus II. Stowed away aboard the cargo ship Laden, Blue Team infiltrated the heavily-fortified rebel facility and retrieved Watts, with minimal complications and injuries.

## OPERATION: FALLEN WALLS

The Spartan-IIs tirelessly engaged the Covenant threat on every front, even as the enemy carved a path toward humanity's Inner Colonies. Although the Spartans had seen a handful of victories, Operation: FALLEN WALLS (February 9-12, 2535) marked the last attempt by the UNSC to hold colonies and risk Spartans after losing orbital superiority. In this operation, SPARTAN-II operatives on Jericho VII led the successful UNSC counterattacks on Covenant landing zones until the alien forces commenced plasma bombardment on their own positions and troops after forcing the Navy to retreat.

# SPARTAN-II

## DATES ACTIVE:
2513–CURRENT

## PROJECT LEAD:
DR. CATHERINE HALSEY

## PROJECT SPONSOR:
UEG \\ UNSC \\ Navy \\ ONI \\ Section Three \\ ASTER

## BACKGROUND:
Initially classified as "ORION Generation II," ONI commissioned a new super-soldier project in 2513. Dr. Halsey was recruited to run both the new Project: Spartan-II and associated Project: Mjolnir. Strategic assessment of the Insurrection campaign indicated that the continuance of human civilization was threatened, and all ethical and legal restrictions on candidate selection, education, and medical protocols were removed, as the SPARTAN-II augmentation protocols required both a very specific genetic profile and adolescent candidates. Between 2516 and 2517, seventy-five young candidates were selected and brought to Reach for indoctrination and training. These details are not included in public revelations of the program authorized in 2547.

## DEPLOYMENT:
Integration of gene therapy, musculo-skeletal modifications, cybernetic implants, and transgenic hybridization proved far more challenging than originally estimated. Only thirty-three of the candidates passed the initial augmentation process without major trauma or death. After successful field trials, the Spartan-IIs were paired with the first generation of Mjolnir powered assault armor and executing combat operations against Covenant forces within weeks of first contact. Additional rehabilitated candidates were brought into operational condition between 2526 and 2530.

## RESULTS:
Despite their low absolute numbers, the strategic value of the Spartan-II candidates has proved impossible to calculate. Even quantitative analysis of their kill ratio of Insurrection and Covenant forces defies any historical comparison or analysis. Conservative estimates place the overall value of each Spartan-II during the Covenant War as equivalent to the combat power of an entire Sector Fleet.

# SPARTAN-III AUGMENTATION

## PROGRAM ORIGINS

Despite the profound success achieved by the SPARTAN-II program, a lack of trust in Halsey's loyalty, concerns with cost and reproducibility, as well as an apprehension with Covenant's seeming invincibility, led to a new super-soldier proposal by Colonel James Ackerson on October 24, 2531. Leaning heavily on research pioneered for SPARTAN-II and ORION, Ackerson promised lower costs, higher personnel yields, and more immediate support for the war.

ONI approved this effort, and on December 27, 2531, Alpha Company—the first collection of SPARTAN-III candidates— arrived on the remote world of Onyx. They would be trained by Lieutenant Colonel Kurt Ambrose and Senior Chief Petty Officer Franklin Mendez at ONI's Camp Currahee complex.

## TRAINING REGIME

The SPARTAN-III training regimen mirrored that of SPARTAN-II, with intensive physical conditioning and education conducted by hand-picked trainers and multiple on-site AI. Unlike ORION and SPARTAN-II, this training was not supplemented by general education or development of skills that lacked an immediate military application. All training and indoctrination emphasized the significance of achieving objectives at any cost and a willingness to sacrifice for the UNSC.

## ALPHA COMPANY

Alpha Company candidates were brought to the remote world of Onyx on December 27, 2531. Their first combat deployment was Operation: FIREBRAND on October 16, 2535, where they suppressed an anti-UEG coup d'état on Mamore. Later operations include Operation: IRON GREAVE on New Constantinople and Operation: HWACHA counter-boarding actions against Covenant forces in the Bonanza fleet action.

Alpha Company's final deployment was Operation: PROMETHEUS, on June 27, 2537. Alpha Company Spartan-III's were assigned to sabotage a heavily defended Covenant shipyard discovered near UEG space. Though their mission was a success, the surviving Spartan-III's were cut off from their exfiltration craft and destroyed by Covenant reinforcements. There were no survivors, apart from a handful of special candidates previously reassigned to different units by Colonel Ackerson.

# SPARTAN-III

## DATES ACTIVE:
2531–CURRENT

## PROJECT LEAD:
COLONEL JAMES ACKERSON

## PROJECT SPONSOR:
UEG \\ UNSC \\ Navy \\ ONI \\ Section Three \\ CHRYSANTHEMUM

## BACKGROUND:

An attempt to create large numbers of Spartans in a short period of time, SPARTAN-III transformed orphaned children into a new breed of super-soldier using streamlined biological augmentation processes paired with experimental biochemical enhancement. ONI approved the project in 2431, and all ethical and legal waivers from SPARTAN-II were retained for this work. Candidates were chosen from young war orphans, organized into large companies that underwent augmentation as soon as their bodies would accept it. Augmentation success was roughly 60 percent in 2536 but rose to nearly 100 percent by 2552.

## DEPLOYMENT:

The first company of three hundred Spartan-III super-soldiers was deployed in 2536. After demonstrating their combat capabilities, the UNSC deployed the entire company for Operation: PROMETHEUS. Though an unqualified success, there were no survivors. A second company graduated in 2545 and was destroyed during Operation: TORPEDO. A third company was formed but were deployed too late in the war to see action.

## RESULTS:

Though losses were extraordinarily high, the UNSC was willing to trade casualties for time at this stage of the Covenant War, and the SPARTAN-III successes in PROMETHEUS and TORPEDO were judged to be well worth the cost. The SPARTAN-III augmentation process also showed great promise for further development, with selection parameters for the bioaugmentation protocols greatly expanding over the years. The third company of SPARTAN-IIIs has now been reorganized under the Spartan branch or placed in reserve status, but side effects of their prototype augmentations require additional medical monitoring and surgeries to make them compatible with Spartan-IV protocols.

# SPARTAN-IV AUGMENTATION

## STANDARDS OF EXCELLENCE

SPARTAN-IV recruits are drawn from experienced personnel in every branch of UNSC service, selecting individuals voluntarily who possessed exceptional willpower, focus, and bravery, while also meeting the precise physiological requirements for the cybernetic and biological augmentation procedures. Joining the Spartan branch is an honor, a privilege, and a heavy burden: even the most battle-hardened veteran is rarely prepared for the intensity and tempo of missions expected of elite super-soldier cadres.

## STOLEN GAUNTLET

Nevertheless, SPARTAN-IV selection process is not foolproof. SPARTAN-IV are soldiers with preexisting philosophies and loyalties, and even the most carefully screened candidate can react to their augmentation and training in unexpected ways. Individual Spartans represent a strategically significant level of combat power and pose a major security threat if their loyalty is compromised. The STOLEN GAUNTLET fail-safe protocol has been created to provides training and permissive rules of engagement for special agents tasked with tracking down and swiftly neutralizing rogue Spartans.

# SPARTAN-IV

**DATES ACTIVE:**
2550–CURRENT

**PROJECT LEAD:**
REAR ADMIRAL MUSA GHANEM

**PROJECT SPONSOR:**
UEG \\ UNSC \\ Navy \\ ONI \\ Section Three \\ ORCHID

## BACKGROUND:

Spartan-IV is a revision and expansion of the ORION augmentation protocols using biological, chemical, and cybernetic enhancement methods developed for Spartan-II and Spartan-III. Initially an experiment to add limited enhancements to ONI special forces operators, the new technology proved that adult candidates could be physically augmented to within an order of magnitude of the capabilities of a Spartan-II with less than three months of surgeries and acclimation. Paired with the second-generation Mjolnir powered assault armor, the combination was more cost effective than Spartan-III, without the ethical complications. The first Spartan-IV candidates underwent augmentation in 2552, in the closing weeks of the Covenant War.

## DEPLOYMENT:

Spartan-IV recruits are drawn from UNSC veterans, selecting from among volunteers who possess exceptional willpower, focus, and bravery, while also meeting the precise physiological requirements for the cybernetic and biological augmentation procedures. All candidates undergo extensive psychological evaluation and post-augmentation monitoring. Spartan-IV augmentation is meta-stable and requires periodic maintenance to avoid performance degradation and potential health complications.

## RESULTS:

Spartan-IV is considered a major success and is now a cornerstone of UEG defense policy and UNSC strategic planning. It has produced a substantial number of super-soldiers capable of exacting the UNSC's efforts at key junctures in the post-war arena, including counter-Insurrection operations and combat missions against Covenant remnants. Large-scale Spartan-IV detachments on expeditionary warships such as the UNSC *Infinity* have proven to be essential strategic assets, especially given the challenging astro-political landscape.

UNITED NATIONS SPACE COMMAND

## PART 06
# BATTLEFRONTS

In the aftermath of the Covenant War, Spartans have been deployed to every corner of the human sphere. As the astro-political situation evolves, you will need to familiarize yourself with the details of every potential enemy faction, their technology, and the key strategic locations they hold. Modern wars stretch across star systems, and your knowledge base must be far-reaching.

# THE FRONTIER

Many corners of the galaxy remain uncharted. Part of your mandate as a Spartan-IV is not only to protect the worlds currently under humanity's control but also to help the UEG expand humanity's influence into more distant corners of the galaxy. Your predecessors have fought in engagements on more planets than any other force in human history, and you will likely continue that legacy. Do not think of these potential deployment zones as dots on a map, or stars in the sky. Think of them as your territory. And Spartans do not give up their territory without a fight.

# DOISAC

### JIRALHANAE HOMEWORLD

### ENVIRONMENT:
TERRESTRIAL, HAZARDOUS, DEVELOPED

### STRATEGIC SIGNIFICANCE:
MEDIUM

### THREAT LEVEL:
DELTA

## OVERVIEW:
The UNSC's knowledge of the remote planet of Doisac is limited. The Jiralhanae (better known as "Brutes" to UNSC soldiers) population is extraordinarily aggressive and well-armed, and extreme caution is advised at all times in any dealings with their clans and warlords. The Brute homeworld itself is utterly lethal to most humans, due to the local wildlife, roving Brute packs, and lingering radiological contamination from their pre-Covenant world wars.

## TERRAIN:
Doisac and its moons are bases of operation for most of the pirates and reavers currently operating in the Orion Arm of the galaxy. Recent intelligence indicates that an unusual level of power consolidation and cooperation has begun unifying the previously independent Brute packs, which ONI attributes to the influence of warlords associated with the Banished.

## MISSIONS:
Conditions on the surface of Doisac are of priority interest to ONI, and political disruption or targeted strikes may be necessary to prevent the reemergence of a unified Jiralhanae military threat. Spartans are on alert that operations in Jiralhanae territory are currently being planned to further assess the situation.

# EARTH

## UEG CAPITAL

### ENVIRONMENT:
TERRESTRIAL, GARDEN, DEVELOPED

### STRATEGIC SIGNIFICANCE:
CRITICAL

### THREAT LEVEL:
ALPHA

### GRANT

It doesn't have perfect defenses to be sure, but Earth does get an outsized share of the UNSCs strength.

## OVERVIEW:
Nine thousand years after the dawn of human civilization and somehow Earth still endures, and that is in no small part due to the actions of Spartans. As the birthplace of humanity and the heart of both our civil and military command structure, Earth remains the most strategically significant location in the human sphere.

## TERRAIN:
Earth and Sol system habitats are defended by a vast network of orbital weapon platforms, naval flotillas, and slipspace tracking stations. Although the system is by no means unassailable, few enemy fleets have the strength in either numbers or firepower to risk an incursion. Most Spartan missions on Earth involve strikes against Insurrection groups and bodyguard duty for high-importance personnel.

## MISSIONS:
The majority of Spartans on Earth are assigned to Joint Task Force MARIAH, which is responsible for site security at the Forerunner portal complex near Voi, in the East African Protectorate. MARIAH has requested that Spartans with experience with Forerunner facilities be detached from the *Infinity* for a special reconnaissance operation deeper into the facility. Contact Spartan Commander Palmer if you would like to volunteer for this rare pathfinder opportunity.

# KAMCHATKA

## COVENANT STAGING AREA

### ENVIRONMENT:
TERRESTRIAL, COLD, UNDEVELOPED

### STRATEGIC SIGNIFICANCE:
HIGH

### THREAT LEVEL:
DELTA

## OVERVIEW:
Kamchatka is located in the remote Caspar star system and is a primary staging area for Jul 'Mdama's Covenant forces. Its full significance to the Covenant is not yet known, though ONI surveys have revealed extensive exotic mineral resources and the presence of large, unidentified, Forerunner complexes beneath the surface.

## TERRAIN:
Though the planet initially appears to be an unremarkable, barely habitable arctic world, closer analysis has revealed evidence of extensive mega-engineering of the planet by the Forerunners for unknown reasons. The planet's surface is rugged, with much of the surface covered by ice and snow.

## MISSIONS:
In recent weeks the bulk of Jul 'Mdama's fleet has consolidated at Kamchatka for an unknown reason. The concentration of Covenant forces and ONI-flagged high-value targets presents a unique opportunity, and the UNSC *Infinity* has been ordered to immediately launch a strike against Covenant leadership known to be at the location.

# MERIDIAN

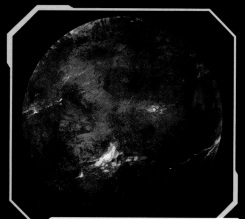

## RESOURCE OUTPOST

### ENVIRONMENT:
TERRESTRIAL, HOT, GLASSED

### STRATEGIC SIGNIFICANCE:
HIGH

### THREAT LEVEL:
CHARLIE

### THORNE

Liang-Dortmund is strip mining a war grave. It's disgusting, but the megacorporations only care about profits, and the UEG will do anything to rebuild its industry.

## OVERVIEW:
Meridian was attacked and subjected to extensive plasma bombardment during the Covenant War, which has rendered it almost uninhabitable, but it is no less a part of the Unified Earth Government. Meridian is the focus of a controversial program by the Liang-Dortmund megacorporation to mine the glassed surface for refined metals and clear wreckage for an ambitious environmental rehabilitation and re-terraforming program.

## TERRAIN:
Meridian is classified as a hazardous environment. The surface is subject to extreme atmospheric phenomena such as lighting tempests, glass storms, and fire whirls. The planet is tectonically unstable and volcanically active.

## MISSIONS:
Spartan Operations has been alerted that unusual energy anomalies recently detected beneath the surface may indicate unauthorized use of Forerunner technology by Liang-Dortmund. ONI has notified the UNSC *Infinity* that Spartan Fireteams may be requested for an investigation.

# REACH

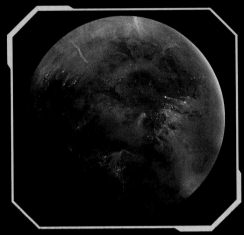

## FORMER UNSC FORTRESS WORLD

### ENVIRONMENT:
TERRESTRIAL, COLD, GLASSED

### STRATEGIC SIGNIFICANCE:
LOW

### THREAT LEVEL:
BRAVO

### GRANT
The Reavians (local colonists) were a hardy bunch. And loyal to the UEG, for all that mattered in the end.

## OVERVIEW:
Reach was the most developed and populous colony in the UEG until it was attacked in the final days of the Covenant War. Though classed as a priority redevelopment area after the war, all major military sites and population centers are damaged or destroyed, and UNSC presence is currently minimal. Operations on Reach are under strict ONI security classification and should not be discussed with other UNSC personnel, regardless of their rank or position.

## TERRAIN:
Reach suffered damage to its biosphere during the Covenant attack but remains habitable. Terrestrial and orbital operations are complicated by the presence of unaffiliated local civilians, UEG contractors, and unlicensed Kig-Yar salvagers.

## MISSIONS:
Specific strategic objectives are classified, but Spartans with combat engineering experience and covert action backgrounds have been asked to report to ONI for screening and assessment.

### THORNE
Rumor is that ONI is sending us in to scour the area around the old UNSC headquarters complex under Menachite Mountain. What are they looking for in the rubble?

# SANGHELIOS

## SANGHEILI HOMEWORLD

## ENVIRONMENT:
TERRESTRIAL, HOT, DEVELOPED

## STRATEGIC SIGNIFICANCE:
CRITICAL

## THREAT LEVEL:
CHARLIE

### THORNE

Thel 'Vadam killed millions when he served the Covenant. But he also was the Master Chief's ally at the end of the war. I'm not sure what to think about him.

## OVERVIEW:
Sanghelios is the homeworld of the alien Sangheili, or "Elites" as they are often referred. The world was recently united under the leadership of the Arbiter, Thel 'Vadam, but tensions remain high. The Arbiter's Swords of Sanghelios faction is an ally of the UNSC, but his forces are ambivalent to human strategic and political goals.

## TERRAIN:
By human standards, Sanghelios is not an ideal world, with extraordinarily dangerous wildlife and a harsh climate heavily influenced by the star system's twin suns. The planet has a substantial number of Forerunner sites, many of which are located at the center of important shrines and religious centers. UNSC forces are not permitted in these areas without a Swords of Sanghelios escort.

## MISSIONS:
Sanghelios is currently under siege by Covenant forces led by Jul 'Mdama, and most of the planet's city-states have experienced heavy fighting. The Arbiter has not requested UNSC support, but the *Infinity* has received a warning order that military intervention in support of the Swords of Sanghelios may be necessary. Due to the complicated social dynamics of the Sangheili, Spartans with xenoanthropological experience are preferred for liaison and scout missions on the planet.

# THE HALO ARRAY

## WEAPON RINGS

### ENVIRONMENT:
TERRESTRIAL, VARIES, ARTIFICIAL

### STRATEGIC SIGNIFICANCE:
SUPREME

### THREAT LEVEL:
DELTA

### GRANT
Dangerous or not, a
Halo visit is on my
bucket list.

## OVERVIEW:
Each ringworld in the Halo Array is 10,000 kilometers (6,213 miles) in diameter. Their inner surfaces are sculpted with mountains and valleys, covered by water and vegetation, and stocked with animals. This thin layer of life on each ring conceals machinery for spreading death at a galactic scale. Under the surface, there are generators and focusing arrays designed to create a wave of energy that kills all sentient creatures as part of the Forerunner's plan to stop the parasitical Flood.

## TERRAIN:
With only two of the Array's six remaining rings located, the UNSC has prepared quick-reaction plans to secure and disable these installations as soon as they are found. Each Halo houses billions of mechanized Sentinel constructs and is home to any number of uncategorized life-forms that were stored on the ring for safekeeping, all of which may prove dangerous if encountered. War Games provides the perfect environment to test and familiarize Spartans with the structures and enemies that could be encountered on-site.

## MISSIONS:
It is standing UNSC policy that securing the firing mechanism of Halo rings (known as an Activation Index) is of the highest priority. Spartan-IVs are under standing orders to use any means necessary to prevent or delay the activation of Halo, and the deployment of weapons of mass destruction on the rings is preemptively authorized. Due to the high probability of Flood parasite samples being stored on a Halo, all missions to their surface must be undertaken with the most severe biohazard precautions.

# STRATEGIC RING LOCATIONS

## LIBRARY:

The Library is an archive that contains information about species stored on the ring—past and present—and holds the Activation Index. The Activation Index is a key needed to authorize the ring's firing sequence. Locating the Library and removing the Activation Index is a high-priority task assigned to Spartans.

## CONTROL ROOM:

The Control Room is where all high-level surveys of the ring's functions can be conducted. If the Activation Index is available, the Control Room is where the ring's firing sequence is initiated.

## SILENT CARTOGRAPHER:

The ring's map room is often the first strategic structure identified on the ring. Securing it can make locating the Library and Control Room much easier.

## FLOOD STORAGE:

Every ring encountered by humanity has had at least one major Flood storage site containing live samples. These facilities were used in the vain search for a way to defeat the Flood, and in some cases the parasite has managed to escape containment. Spartan crisis action teams with specialized anti-Flood equipment and training are the only UNSC forces authorized to enter these areas.

## PULSE GENERATORS:

If the ring is activated it will destroy all thinking life in a 25,000-light-year radius around the installation and trigger the other rings around the galaxy to fire. The ring's "Halo Effect" is generated by a network of powerful generators placed around the ring. In the event of imminent activation, these generators can be targeted to slow or stop the ring from firing.

## SENTINEL FACTORIES:

Beneath the surface are vast assembly areas which construct the billions of Sentinel automated drones who maintain and defend the ring. These areas typically lack gravity or an atmosphere.

# THE HALO ARRAY

There are seven Halo rings in their full configuration, located throughout the galaxy in a pattern that guarantees total coverage by their energy pulse in the event of activation. With the disappearance of Gamma Halo in 2557, the locations and status of only two Halo other rings are currently known. Any information related to the location of a Halo ring is to be forwarded to ONI immediately.

> **THORNE**
>
> I've been told you can travel to the Ark, though it's a complicated slipspace route, but the trip can take a couple of years. Yeah, let's stick to the portals.

## INSTALLATION 00 – THE ARK // STATUS: ACTIVE.

Installation 00 is the factory and control nexus for the Halo Array. The Ark is located outside of the Milky Way Galaxy so it can stay out of firing range of the Halo Array and can only be reached via slipspace portal complexes, such as the one discovered on Earth in 2552. The scientific and military outpost on the Ark continues to explore the massive Forerunner facility in order to determine a way to shut down the remaining Halo rings.

## INSTALLATION 01 – BETA SITE // STATUS: UNKNOWN.

Information on Installation 01 is limited to data recovered by the Master Chief during his brief visit to Installation 00's Control Room. Intelligence collected there appears to show that the ring is no longer habitable, though this information may be outdated or misleading.

## INSTALLATION 02 – EPSILON SITE // STATUS: UNKNOWN.

Recovered Forerunner records from the Ark indicate that Installation 02's monitor, 007 Contrite Witness, contacted the Ark for a status update as recently as 2490.

## INSTALLATION 03 – GAMMA SITE // STATUS: UNKNOWN.

Installation 03 was formerly located in the Khaprae system and was the site of a large UEG and UNSC detachment studying its functions and recovering artifacts. In early 2557 the ring traveled through slipspace to an unknown destination. ONI retains custody of the ring's Activation Index at an undisclosed location.

## INSTALLATION 04 – ALPHA SITE // STATUS: DESTROYED.

Alpha Halo was the first Halo ring to be discovered. After the ring's firing mechanism was inadvertently triggered, it was destroyed by the Master Chief. The presence of Flood and aggressive Sentinels in the ring's debris field in the Soell star system resulted in the area being placed under the UNSC's strictest quarantine restrictions. Despite the hazards, Spartan missions have recently been undertaken on the nearby moon of Basis.

## INSTALLATION 05 – DELTA SITE // STATUS: QUARANTINED.

Installation 05 was the site of the most decisive actions of the Covenant War. The release of the Flood Gravemind hidden within it challenged the might of the Covenant, even as political strife over how to use the ancient ring broke the ancient alliances that held its member species together. The ring and the Coelest star system was quarantined after the war, and both UNSC and Swords of Sanghelios warships patrol the region. The status of the ring's Activation Index is unknown.

## INSTALLATION 06 – KAPPA SITE // STATUS: UNKNOWN.

The location of Installation 06 is unknown, though it appears to be fully functional based on analysis of the encrypted Forerunner status reports found on Installation 00.

## INSTALLATION 07 – ZETA SITE // STATUS: ACTIVE.

Zeta Site was one of two Halo rings on which the UEG had established a scientific outpost. Strange and alien, even in comparison to Alpha, Delta, and Gamma, the Zeta ring was difficult to analyze, and its caretaker protocols are impossible to predict or control. The ring's Monitor and Library facility have not been located, leaving many questions unanswered as to the function and role of the ring within the larger Halo array. A large military and scientific contingent currently occupies Zeta Site.

## INSTALLATION 08 – ALPHA REPLACEMENT // DESTROYED.

Installation 08 was produced by the Ark to replace the ring destroyed by the Master Chief. Incomplete and unstable, the Chief used the Activation Index previously recovered from Alpha Halo to prematurely activate it above the Ark, destroying the Flood infection that had spread throughout the extragalactic facility. Nothing remains of this installation, as the Ark used the wreckage for its own repairs.

## INSTALLATION 09 – ALPHA REPLACEMENT // STATUS: UNKNOWN.

The last status update from the Ark research base indicated that another ring had entered production within Installation 00's massive forges. The status of this new ring is currently unknown.

UNSC

UNITED NATIONS SPACE COMMAND

PART 07

# SPARTAN DOSSIERS

# SPARTAN LEGENDS

As a Spartan, you stand on the shoulders of giants, and your successes can only further enhance our shared legacy. When a Spartan enters the battlefronts, they will be expected to live up to the high standard set by those who have come before.

# SPARTAN LEGENDS

## MASTER CHIEF PETTY OFFICER JOHN-117

### SPARTAN LEGEND

LOADOUT: CUSTOM GEN2 MARK VI AND MA5D ASSAULT RIFLE
SERVICE NUMBER: NONSTANDARD ID S-117
BACKGROUND: UNSC NAVY \\ BLUE TEAM
BIRTHWORLD: ERIDANUS II
HEIGHT: 2180 MM (7FT 2IN)
WEIGHT: 130 KG (287 LB)

A Demon to the Covenant. Hero to the UNSC. The discoverer of the Halo rings. The man who won the Covenant War. No matter how you refer to him, the Master Chief is inarguably the best Spartan to ever wear the Mjolnir armor and take up the fight to protect humanity. But the Master Chief is not simply a warrior, he is also a statesman who has turned enemies in allies, and a scholar who has learned much of the ancient Forerunners.

# THE LEGEND

Master Chief Petty Officer John-117 is the quintessential Spartan. He is a living legend, inspiring awe like a mythological hero from ancient history, but with the formative presence of an armored tank. Throughout his extensive military career, John-117 has accomplished feats and displayed a kind of undaunted courage that is nothing short of extraordinary. Long years of war, however, have given the Master Chief a somber and serious mode of thought. Though his stance and posture can be at ease, the Chief is always alert: ready to launch into action at a moment's notice.

Proficient in all aspects of infantry tactics as well as the basics of zero-to-low gravity aerospace combat, one of John-117's most notable skills is leadership—his ability to effectively direct operational detachments ranging in size from Spartan Fireteams to full-strength Marine battalions. It has been noted that UNSC personnel at all levels generally defer to John-117's experience and strategic intellect, oftentimes giving him a level of authority that far outstrips his actual rank.

# MASTER CHIEF'S KEY VICTORIES

As of August 2558, John-117 had completed 209 individual, recorded military operations (136 full campaigns) during the Insurrection and the Covenant War, including operations, which occurred after the three-decades long conflict. Like a handful of other Spartans, the Master Chief has received every single major service medal except for the Prisoner of War Medallion. He is arguably the most pivotal and important figure of humanity in the 26th century, though many of his feats are not part of official military records.

**STRIKES AGAINST THE INSURRECTION (SEPTEMBER 2525):** Master Chief's first recorded mission. Led an operation deep in enemy territory to capture a dangerous Insurrection leader at Eridanus Secundus.

**FIRST COUNTERATTACK AGAINST THE COVENANT (APRIL 2526):** Rescue mission on Circinius IV. Despite heavy Covenant opposition, the Master Chief and Blue Team rescued many cadets from the besieged Corbulo Academy of Military Science on Circinius IV.

**DEFENSE OF REACH (AUGUST 2552):** Information denial operations. Led successful pinpoint strikes in Reach orbit to prevent the Covenant fleet from discovering the location of remaining UEG colonies.

**DISCOVERY OF ALPHA HALO (SEPTEMBER 2552):** Guerrilla warfare. Discovered the first installation of an ancient Forerunner super-weapon array known as Halo. After the installation was activated, he single-handedly sabotaged the ring, destroying it and an entire fleet of Covenant warships.

**BATTLE OF THE ARK (NOVEMBER 2552):** Joint operations. The Master Chief led a coalition of UNSC and Sangheili forces to the extragalactic Ark to finally end the Covenant War in our favor. Was declared Missing in Action (MIA) at the conclusion of the war.

**REQUIEM (JULY 2557):** The Master Chief was recovered on the Forerunner shield world of Requiem after four years. After the Forerunner commander imprisoned in the facility was released, the Master Chief led a successful mission that eliminated the threat before Earth could suffer heavy damage.

# BLUE TEAM

Blue Team is widely considered the most successful strike team in the history of the UNSC. Records indicate that as of 2553, the team had logged more than 220 military operations since the activation of Spartan-II assets in 2525. The exact number is disputed, however, because of the irregular roster that Blue Team (and all Spartan teams) had endured over its four decades of activity. Nevertheless, most would not argue the impact of Blue Team during the course of the Covenant War.

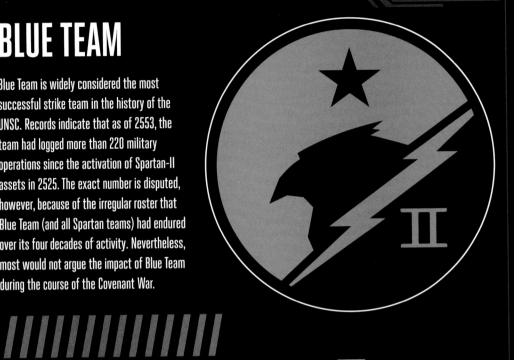

## LIEUTENANT FREDERIC-104

LOADOUT: CUSTOM GEN2 CENTURION AND M395 DMR
SERVICE NUMBER: NONSTANDARD ID S-104
BACKGROUND: UNSC NAVY \\ BLUE TEAM
BIRTHWORLD: BALLAST
HEIGHT: 2163 MM (7 FT 1 IN)
WEIGHT: 132 KG (291 LB)

Musculature aside, Frederic-104 could pass as a tall civilian in certain contexts (such as low-gravity colonies), though he still retains the pale skin, accentuated eye color, and a number of other characteristics attributed to SPARTAN-II biological and cybernetic augmentation. While there is little doubt as to Frederic-104's skill in combat, his true genius lies in strategy, information management, and the forging of different combat elements into a single warfighting force.

# PETTY OFFICER KELLY-087

LOADOUT: CUSTOM GEN2 HERMES AND CUSTOM M45 SHOTGUN "OATHSWORN"
SERVICE NUMBER: NONSTANDARD ID S-087
BACKGROUND: UNSC NAVY \\ BLUE TEAM
BIRTHWORLD: IMBER
HEIGHT: 2110 MM (6 FT 11 IN)
WEIGHT: 112 KG (247 LB)

Even among her super-human Spartan-II peers, Kelly-087 was notable for having the quickest reflexes, even before her exposure to the Mjolnir mobility systems. Kelly-087's speed only increased as her acclimation to the Mjolnir armor and her biological augmentations were further refined and improved. Kelly-087's remarkable reflexes were honed during childhood training through her frequent participation in twitch-response drills and Zen "no-thought" marksmanship practice.

# PETTY OFFICER LINDA-058

LOADOUT: CUSTOM GEN2 ARGUS AND CUSTOM SRS99-S5 SNIPER RIFLE "NORNFANG"
SERVICE NUMBER: NONSTANDARD ID S-058
BACKGROUND: UNSC NAVY \\ BLUE TEAM
BIRTHWORLD: VERENT
HEIGHT: 2130 MM (7 FT)
WEIGHT: 110 KG (242 LB)

Throughout her career, Linda-058 was employed as a scout-sniper providing long-range combat support and forward observation capabilities for the other members of Blue Team. Her independent streak and unwavering confidence meant that Linda-058 could also be effectively deployed for long periods of time on "lone wolf" missions, operating well outside the boundaries of a traditional structure command environment. Linda-058's skill with long-range weapons is effectively unparalleled, and she's considered one of the UNSC's most talented snipers.

# SERGEANT MAJOR
# AVERY JOHNSON

## WAR HERO

SERVICE NUMBER: 48789-20114-AJ
BACKGROUND: UNSC MARINE CORPS \\ RAIDERS (ORION)
BIRTHWORLD: EARTH
HEIGHT: 1872 MM (6 FT 2 IN)
WEIGHT: 95.5 KG (211 LB)

If it wasn't obvious from his long list of accomplishments and decorations, it is now official that Sergeant Major Avery Johnson was one of the first Spartans, an ORION operative who demonstrated the best that the UNSC can produce in both his leadership and combat ability. Recognized by the Master Chief himself for his valor and dedication to humanity, it's now clear that without Sergeant Major Avery Johnson and what he accomplished in his long and storied career, not only would Spartan branch not exist, humanity wouldn't either.

After decades valiantly leading soldiers in defense of humanity, Johnson would ultimately lose his life in a battle against the rampant Forerunner AI 343 Guilty Spark during the battle on the Ark. Yet his sacrifice would help protect humanity from the threat of the Flood and the galaxy-spanning destruction of the Halo Array, and his example is one that all Spartans—past and present—can learn from.

# DR. CATHERINE HALSEY

## LEAD SCIENTIST FOR PROJECT: SPARTAN-II AND PROJECT: MJOLNIR

SERVICE NUMBER: CIVILIAN CONTRACTOR 409871
BACKGROUND: ONI \\ SECTION THREE
BIRTHWORLD: ENDYMION
HEIGHT: 1702 MM (5 FT 7 IN)
WEIGHT: 53 KG (117 LB)

Dr. Catherine Halsey is without a doubt one of the most stunning human intellects of the 26th century, with the highest record General Cognitive Propensity (GCP) score recorded in over five centuries. Her brilliance was a significant factor in the success of SPARTAN-II and MJOLNIR, two revolutionary projects, which ultimately ensured the survival of humanity in the face of the Covenant. The extensive knowledge she has accrued of the Covenant and the Forerunners has often placed her at critical junctures in humanity's development, even though her brash and often incendiary attitude is considered a major liability by the Office of Naval Intelligence (ONI) who employs her. Though she is neither a Spartan nor part of the official UNSC command hierarchy, Dr. Catherine Halsey's influence on the UEG's scientific efforts is unparalleled, and her contributions to the development of the Spartan branch are undeniable. Her current status is classified.

## INFINITY SPARTANS

# SPARTAN SARAH PALMER

## SPARTAN COMMANDER, UNSC INFINITY

LOADOUT: GEN2 SCOUT AND DUAL M6H MAGNUMS
SERVICE NUMBER: 65287-98303-SP
BACKGROUND: UNSC MARINE CORPS \\ ODST
BIRTHWORLD: LUNA
HEIGHT: 2057 MM (6 FT 9 IN)
WEIGHT: 109.3 KG (241 LB)

> **GRANT**
>
> Uhm. In case it needs to be said, don't let the Commander know we're gossiping behind her back.

A former ODST who devoted her life to taking down Covenant, Palmer demonstrates nearly every attribute Jun was looking for as he assembled the first class of potential Spartan-IV super-soldiers. She is fearless, determined, intelligent, and handy with a Magnum. Palmer serves as Spartan Commander aboard the UNSC *Infinity* and is the senior *Spartan for Expeditionary Strike Group One* (ESG 1).

> **GRANT**
>
> Commander Palmer has never quite given up being an ODST. She still tries to lead from the front and put some lead down-range at every chance. The Captain must have a hell of a time making sure she actually stays on the bridge and doesn't sneak into a drop pod during every mission.

> **THORNE**
>
> She seems a lot . . . calmer after our recent adventures at that Forerunner data archive. Captain Lasky making her the acting XO of the ship also seems to have done wonders in getting her to focus on the big picture.

# INFINITY SPARTANS

# SPARTAN GABRIEL THORNE

## SPARTAN FIRETEAM LEADER, MAJESTIC

LOADOUT: GEN2 RECRUIT AND MA5D ASSAULT RIFLE
SERVICE NUMBER: 83920-91083-GT
BACKGROUND: UNSC ARMY \\ RIFLEMAN
BIRTHWORLD: EARTH
HEIGHT: 2081 MM (6 FT 10 IN)
WEIGHT: 123.4 KG (272 LB)

Born on Earth to a family with a strong tradition of service, Gabriel Thorne enlisted in the UNSC Army shortly before the end of the Covenant War. Participating in some of the desperate final battles of that war, Thorne was defending the last redoubts of humanity on Mars when news arrived that the conflict was over—ended by the Master Chief and his ally, the Arbiter. Spartan Gabriel Thorne is currently in command of Fireteam Majestic, aboard the UNSC *Infinity*.

| GRANT | THORNE | GRANT |
|---|---|---|
| 123.4 kg? More like 130 kg. | Oh, you want to play that game, Grant? | Kidding! Kidding! |

# FIRETEAM MAJESTIC /////////////////

Fireteam Majestic is one of the most decorated Spartan-IV Fireteams stationed on UNSC *Infinity*. Majestic was heavily involved in the campaign on Requiem in 2558 as well as the pursuit of Jul 'Mdama's forces.

## SPARTAN TEDRA GRANT

LOADOUT: GEN2 PATHFINDER AND M395 DMR
SERVICE NUMBER: 95984-78393-TG
BACKGROUND: UNSC NAVY \\ MILITARY POLICE
BIRTHWORLD: ARCADIA
HEIGHT: 2060 MM (6 FT 9 IN)
WEIGHT: 108.4 KG (239 LB)

### GRANT

I swear, I didn't touch up this bio at all . . . okay, maybe a little.

Although an all-round remarkable Spartan, Grant's best talents are her sharp insight and clear decision-making. She remains calm and devoted to the task at hand, no matter how harried the situation may be.

## SPARTAN CARLO HOYA

LOADOUT: GEN2 OPERATOR AND M45D SHOTGUN
SERVICE NUMBER: 90302-89202-CH
BACKGROUND: UNSC MARINES \\ ODST
BIRTHWORLD: ASMARA
HEIGHT: 2161 MM (7 FT 1 IN)
WEIGHT: 127.4 KG (281 LB)

### THORNE

If you need to know anything about CQB tactics, hit up Hoya. He's a walking encyclopedia of ways to take down aliens while up close and personal.

Spartan Hoya is the close-quarters combat specialist of Fireteam Majestic, and his reputation for always finding a way to be in the thick of the action is legendary. Though initially overconfident and brazen, as are many new Spartans, Hoya has learned that aggression does not always equal bravery.

# SPARTAN ANTHONY MADSEN

LOADOUT: GEN2 RECON AND SRS99-S5 SNIPER RIFLE

SERVICE NUMBER: 75283-56282-AM

BACKGROUND: UNSC MARINES \\ FORCE RECON

BIRTHWORLD: NEW LLANELLI

HEIGHT: 2090 MM (6 FT 10 IN)

WEIGHT: 126.1 KG (278 LB)

### THORNE
Can't get him to shut up in the barracks, but he's all business during an op.

The oldest and most experienced member of Fireteam Majestic, Spartan Madsen is a talented soldier and highly skilled marksman. As a Spartan, Madsen prefers to stay in a support role, acting as a mentor and trainer for new Spartan-IVs aboard the UNSC *Infinity* and acting as the second-in-command for Majestic when Spartan Thorne is not available.

# SPARTAN NAIYA RAY

LOADOUT: GEN2 INFILTRATOR & MA5D ASSAULT RIFLE

SERVICE NUMBER: 73993-54580-NR

BACKGROUND: UNSC AIR FORCE \\ SIGNALS INTELLIGENCE

BIRTHWORLD: HEAVENSWARD

HEIGHT: 2130 MM (7 FT)

WEIGHT: 111 KG (245 LB)

### GRANT
What happened to Jacknife is still a sore point among the INFINITY Spartans. I'm sure you're curious, but don't pry into what happened right now. Thanks.

The newest member of Fireteam Majestic, Spartan Ray was transferred from Fireteam Jackknife after the rest of the team was killed in action during the diplomatic mission on Ealen IV. She brings years of experience as a signals intelligence officer, as well as skills gained during a tour of duty as a Headhunter working directly for ONI Section 3.

# SPARTAN OPERATIONS

# JUN-A266

## CHIEF OF STAFF, SPARTANS

LOADOUT: GEN1 SCOUT AND SRS99 SNIPER RIFLE
SERVICE NUMBER: S-A266
BACKGROUND: SPARTAN-III \\ NOBLE TEAM
BIRTHWORLD: NEW HARMONY
HEIGHT: 2116 MM (6 FT 11IN)
WEIGHT: 111.1KG (244 LB)

Though his now wears a business suit rather than Mjolnir powered armor in day-to-day tasks, Jun-A266 is still widely recognized as one of the most talented snipers alive. His attention to detail and extensive combat experience as a core member of the legendary Noble Team is what brought him to the attention of Rear Admiral Musa Ghanem, Commander-in-Chief of the Spartan branch. He serves as a recruiter and operational manager of the Spartan-IV program, reviewing potential Spartan candidates and serving as Ghanem's representative to the UNSC Security Council for routine administrative tasks.

//////////////

# INFINITY SPARTANS

# SPARTAN JAMESON LOCKE

## SPARTAN FIRETEAM LEADER, OSIRIS

LOADOUT: GEN2 HUNTER AND BR85 BATTLE RIFLE
SERVICE NUMBER: 73808-03153-JL
BACKGROUND: ONI \\ SECTION 3
BIRTHWORLD: JERICHO VII
HEIGHT: 2080 MM (6 FT 10 IN)
WEIGHT: 115.7 KG (255 LB)

Most of Spartan Locke's previous life as an ONI operative remains highly classified, but to witness him in the field as an expert tracker, encyclopedic resource on humanity's outer colonies, and a brilliantly calculating soldier is to understand what makes Locke effective in all of these roles. Simply put, he's a problem solver. Since transitioning from spook to Spartan, Locke has taken part in critical missions that have included counterintelligence, colonial integrity, and xenoarchaeological security.

# FIRETEAM OSIRIS /////////////

## SPARTAN EDWARD BUCK

LOADOUT: GEN2 HELLJUMPER AND MA5D ASSAULT RIFLE
SERVICE NUMBER: 92458-37017-EB
BACKGROUND: UNSC MARINES \\ ODST
BIRTHWORLD: DRACO III
HEIGHT: 2057 MM (6 FT 9 IN)
WEIGHT: 112.5 KG (248 LB)

### THORNE

He plays it cool, but one look at his service record and you'll see a greatest hits list of the deadliest Covenant War campaigns.

Edward Buck has long displayed strong leadership skills and perseverance despite participating in some of the Covenant War's most vicious and desperate battles. As a former ODST, Buck has considerable combat experience, but his most valuable contribution to Fireteam Osiris is as a joint-forces liaison and advisor.

## SPARTAN HOLLY TANAKA

LOADOUT: GEN2 TECHNICIAN AND M395 DMR
SERVICE NUMBER: 93312-28001-HT
BACKGROUND: UNSC ARMY \\ COMBAT ENGINEER
BIRTHWORLD: MINAB
HEIGHT: 2007 MM (6 FT 7 IN)
WEIGHT: 108.4 KG (239 LB)

Holly Tanaka serves as the engineering and electronics expert of Fireteam Osiris. Her keen mind and broad experience allow her to discern the function and operation of human, Covenant, and Forerunner devices and traps without the assistance of smart AI analysts.

# SPARTAN OLYMPIA VALE

LOADOUT: GEN2 COPPERHEAD AND DUAL M20 SMGS
SERVICE NUMBER: 93312-28001-HT
BACKGROUND: ONI \\ XENOANTHROPOLOGIST
BIRTHWORLD: LUYTEN
HEIGHT: 2057 MM (6 FT 9 IN)
WEIGHT: 101.6 KG (224 LB)

Fluent in the alien language of the Sangheili and well studied in other alien cultures, Olympia Vale embodies the cunning and intelligence of a true combat innovator. But don't underestimate Vale's qualities as a soldier because of her experience as a diplomat. After her induction into the Spartan-IV ranks, she proved to have a preternatural understanding of military strategy that has helped Spartans fight smarter rather than harder on several vital missions.

PART 08

# UNSC

# ORGANIZATION

# UNITED NATIONS SPACE COMMAND (UNSC)

This section will guide you through the structure of the UNSC and help you understand the role Spartans play within the organization. The United Nations Space Command (UNSC) is the military arm of the Unified Earth Government (UEG). As part of its mandate to defend Earth and its colonies, the UNSC is tasked with the recruitment and training of a military force capable of deploying military and exploratory assets on an interstellar scale.

Spartans are the newest addition to the UNSC order of battle, and we fill a crucial role as Earth's hyper-lethal special forces, few in number, but highly capable and highly mobile. With strategic effectiveness equivalent to entire companies of conventional military forces, a handful of Spartans can be deployed to sway the outcome of entire campaigns.

As orders filter down from UNSC command and into our ranks, there are countless other UNSC commanders, civilian support staff, and even artificial intelligence protocols whose role goes far beyond supporting Spartans. In every fight, the entirety of humanity's military and scientific expertise must work in lockstep to ensure victory. Study the following organization chart, and remember that, as Spartans, we owe these influential members of the UNSC our respect and allegiance.

## HIGH COMMAND
### (HIGHCOM)

| AIR FORCE | ARMY | MARINES | NAVY | ONI | SPARTANS |

# UNSC ORGANIZATION

As of 2558 the UNSC is divided into a joint staff known as High Command (HighCom) and six military departments.

## HIGH COMMAND:

High Command is the executive body of senior military personnel who direct UNSC operations and advise the UEG civilian leadership on defense matters. Their senior leadership is the Security Council, comprised of the senior officer of each military department. High Command is based on Earth, at the Bravo-6 headquarters complex in Sydney, Australia.

## MILITARY DEPARTMENTS:

The six branches of the UNSC are its fighting force, comprised of men and women who take up arms in defense of humanity and swear allegiance to the UEG. These UNSC branches consist of the Air Force, Army, Marine Corps, Navy, Office of Naval Intelligence, and Spartans. Each branch specializes in a specific aspect of modern combat, but when operating together, their synergy greatly multiplies the UNSCs combat power.

# UNSC MISSION

Though amended since it was established in 2163, the UNSC's statement of function can be summarized in two points:

**1: UPHOLD AND ADVANCE THE POLICIES OF THE UNIFIED EARTH GOVERNMENT.**

**2: ENSURE THE SAFETY AND SECURITY OF UNIFIED EARTH GOVERNMENT TERRITORIES, POSSESSIONS, AND AREAS VITAL TO ITS INTERESTS.**

# NAVAL COMMAND AND
# UNIFIED GROUND COMMAND

## UNSC MILITARY FORCES ARE ORGANIZED INTO TWO UNIFIED COMBATANT COMMANDS:

### NAVAL COMMAND (NAVCOM)

Controls all space-based assets and operations. Warships and their associated support assets are organized into battle groups, which are themselves combined into fleets.

### UNIFIED GROUND COMMAND (UNICOM)

Coordinates terrestrial and close-orbit missions. Planetside forces are grouped into task forces that contain ground, air, and maritime combat assets.

# CENTRAL COMMAND

NavCom and UniCom joint task forces are assigned to one of four Central Commands (CentComs), which are responsible for the defense and security of a specific area of human space. These protected territories are known as CentCom Regions, and they follow well-mapped slipspace routes that connect dozens of star systems. Forces assigned to one CentCom cannot be moved to another without the approval of HighCom, so each Region must carefully marshal the limited resources they have available.

# NAVY

In an era where humanity has spread across hundreds of star systems and faces threats on almost as many fronts, the UNSC Navy has become more than a fleet of ships carrying troops and supplies from point to point. In truth, the UNSC fleet is also the central nervous system for humanity, and its ships carry the vital news, data, and personnel through slipspace to connect our distant worlds and habitats together. As threats gather on many fronts, naval battle groups defend our lives, protect invaluable resources, and deliver hope to vulnerable colony worlds.

## FLEET COMMAND (FLEETCOM)

Fleet Command directs the movement and tasking of Navy warships and is the largest and most powerful component of any NavCom grouping. FleetCom rarely interacts with Spartan operations, although you will work with them when directing orbital fire support missions and coordinating for the starside interception of fleeing enemies.

# NAVAL SPECIAL WARFARE (NAVSPECWAR)

Naval Special Warfare Command trains, equips, and oversees Special Forces personnel who operate in support of UNSC space operations. NavSpecWar provides mission parameters, ships, and specialist personnel to support Spartan actions that take place in planetary orbit and deep space.

# NAVY MISSIONS

*Provide naval forces to ensure freedom of access for aerospace and terrestrial operations.*

The Navy is responsible for destroying or suppressing enemy space components, specifically, those attempting to attack UEG commercial or terrestrial holdings. For this purpose, the Navy organizes, trains, and equips space forces to establish local naval superiority in deep space and close orbit. Collateral functions include:

o   Interstellar transportation of UNSC combat assets.

o   Development of doctrine, procedures, and equipment that are of common interest to the Air Force and Marine Corps.

o   Providing forces for joint aerospace and terrestrial operations, in accordance with UNSC doctrines.

o   Coordination with UEG civil agencies for the establishment and maintenance of naval depots and orbital yards.

o   Establishment of emergency military government in designated crisis areas.

# OFFICE OF NAVAL INTELLIGENCE (ONI)

The Office of Naval Intelligence is the military intelligence arm of the UNSC, and its work is critical to the security of the UEG. In addition to collecting information on alien military technology and troop strengths, it protects classified information and funds research and development projects, which are indispensable to the survival of humanity. ONI is an independent military agency, though it has a very close historical and administrative relationship with the Navy.

ONI is the spiritual home of the Spartan program. Scientists and engineers employed by ONI developed every piece of Spartan technology, from physical augmentation protocols to the fusion power plant that drives your Mjolnir armor. Experimental technologies and intelligence provided by ONI will keep you well armed as you are deployed to defend humankind.

# ONI SECTIONS

ONI is organized into internal Sections that specialize in different aspects of intelligence collection, analysis, and dissemination. Within each Section are activities dedicated to long-term taskings and cases related (usually) to their parent group. Contained in each activity are one or more groups, who are small teams given specific tasks related to supporting their activity, Section, and ONI as a whole. Sections One and Section Three work directly with the Spartan branch.

**SECTION ONE:** Section One is responsible for the collection and analysis of naval intelligence. It is the oldest and most "traditional" element of ONI, with offices and functions that predate the formal creation of the UNSC. Section One Sierra is the activity that supports Navy and Spartan operations with ONI personnel who specialize in sensor interpretation, cryptography, and battle network administration.

**SECTION THREE:** Section Three handles special acquisition, research, and development projects for the UNSC, both directly and covertly, through a vast network of front organizations. The internal organization of Section Three is ever-changing as new projects are funded, resources reallocated, and prototypes handed off to corporate partners for mass production. Beta is the activity who leverages the most Spartans, primarily to test new technologies and tactics.

# ONI MISSIONS

*Provide technical capabilities for the support of psychological, information, and cyber operations.*

The Office of Naval Intelligence (ONI) is the preeminent intelligence service within the UEG. For this purpose, the Office of Naval Intelligence organizes, trains, and equips intelligence collection and analysis organizations, which support UNSC and UEG strategic objectives. Collateral functions include:

- Deployment of covert teams for direct action and technical data collection.

- Oversight of the gathering, analysis, and dissemination of national security information from around the UEG.

- Development of doctrine, techniques, and equipment for the collection and exploitation of information in support of UEG security.

- Providing combat support intelligence for UNSC operations.

- Establishment of covert observation systems around enemy colonies and facilities.

# MARINE CORPS

If the Navy serves as the nervous system for the UNSC, then the highly trained members of the Marine Corps are its eyes, ears, and fists. The Marine Corps are the general-purpose combat force of the UNSC, tasked with quickly responding to conflicts across UEG space. Marines often support Spartans in the field, and you will be working closely with this branch of service throughout your career.

When you encounter Marines in the field, you'll see firsthand what makes them an effective fighting force. From sharpshooters to combat engineers and xenolinguists, the Marine Corps trains and equips a diverse fighting force that is capable of fighting any type of interstellar conflict and winning on every battlefield.

# ORBITAL DROP SHOCK TROOPERS (ODST)

Nicknamed "Helljumpers," Orbital Drop Shock Troopers are the rapid reaction force of the UNSC Marine Corps. ODSTs have earned their reputation as the toughest warfighters in the UNSC. ODSTs are deployed via transorbital support interdiction, seated in an armored drop pod and launched from an orbiting Navy vessel in a meteoric descent directly into battle, building up massive amounts of speed and heat as they descend through the atmosphere. Breaking out of a drop pod in the middle of a raging battle is as close to "out of the frying pan and into the fire" as it gets, and these Marines relish the opportunity to do what others fear.

# MARINE CORPS MISSIONS

*Provide combined arms expeditionary forces and security detachments.*

The Marine Corps is responsible for maintaining an expeditionary force in readiness, which can seize and defend terrestrial and extraterrestrial strategic locales in advance of the main UNSC effort. For this purpose, the Marine Corps organizes, trains, and equips land, airborne, and space combined-arms teams capable of rapid deployment by Air Force and Navy assets. Collateral functions include:

○ Enforcement of emergency military law in designated crisis areas.

○ Development of doctrine, procedures, and equipment that are of common interest to the Army and Navy.

○ Furnishing security teams for the protection of UNSC property and high-value personnel.

○ Deployment of security detachments and organizations for service on Navy ships.

○ Development of doctrine, tactics, techniques, and equipment for the rapid deployment and utilization of interstellar combat power.

# ARMY

The Army is the UNSCs most important force for defending the territories in its possession, and it provides the majority of soldiers who fight in ground campaigns. All Army soldiers are trained warfighters, but in times of peace they also provide an invaluable force of engineers, technicians, builders, and designers who perform public works and improve existing colonial infrastructure to support future UNSC deployments. While the Navy, Spartans, and Marine Corps are the tip of the UNSC spear, it is the Army who is the shaft, providing the necessary logistical support and reserve troops needed to sustain long campaigns.

# RANGERS

Army Rangers are an elite cadre of infantry who specialize in long-term counterinsurgency warfare and the support of resistance groups on alien-occupied worlds. The ruthless and indiscriminate attacks by the Covenant made their work difficult, particularly as the Covenant rarely expressed any interest in seizing and holding ground on human colonies, and simply occupied key areas for limited periods, then glassed the planet.

Nevertheless, Ranger snipers and guerrilla teams ensured that the Covenant paid a heavy price for their occupation. In the post-war period, Rangers have transitioned back into their traditional role as long-range scouts, observing enemy forces and placing sensor systems behind enemy lines to aid the broader UNSC effort. Spartans work closely with the local Rangers to defend human settlements from raiders and organized criminal elements, and often rely on their knowledge of the terrain when conducting deep strikes into enemy staging areas on their planet.

# ARMY MISSIONS

*Provide forces for sustained terrestrial combat operations and civil works.*

The Army is responsible for the defense of UEG terrestrial holdings and the occupation of enemy territories. For this purpose, the Army organizes, trains, and equips amphibious, land, and airborne forces to occupy and defend terrestrial sites. Collateral functions include:

○ Conducting civil works that have strategic application, including projects for improvement of navigation and follow-on terraforming.

○ Development of doctrine, procedures, and equipment that are of common interest to the Air Force and Marine Corps.

○ Organization and training of civil defense units ("militias").

○ Providing forces for joint aerospace and space operations, in accordance with UNSC doctrines.

# AIR FORCE

While the Army and Marine Corps seize ground, Spartans strike at enemy landing zones, and the Navy fights in the space between stars, the Air Force controls the skies. Air Force orbital defense satellites and aerospace interceptors are among the first lines of defense for a colony, and their vigilance is crucial to ensuring that threats are detected early and either eliminated or delayed so reinforcements can be requested.

The Air Force works closely with the Spartans in all major campaigns, including the provisioning of special transport capabilities, supply drops behind enemy lines, and close air support against entrenched enemy positions. The Air Force was also the first branch of service to directly collaborate with the Spartan branch, funding a joint-operations laboratory to test novel ways in which super-soldiers can augment their existing capabilities, and certifying Spartans to operate the latest-generation strike fighters.

# CLOSE ORBIT DEFENSE

The Air Force operates a network of quick reaction squadrons on Earth and the Inner Colonies, which are prepped and ready to deploy with atmospheric fighters and military spaceplanes at the first sign of an attack. These interceptors work in conjunction with orbiting surveillance and weapon satellites to delay and attrition an attack, and backstop Navy fleet assets that may be available. The Air Force takes the defense of the skies and near orbit seriously and have amassed an impressive kill ratio against invading Covenant despite their substantial disadvantage in technology and numbers. Most of its atmospheric forces are comprised of unmanned combat air vehicles, such as the F-99 Wombat, which are expendable and can be deployed in large numbers very quickly.

# AIR FORCE MISSIONS

*Provide aerospace defense and conduct space control operations.*

The Air Force is tasked with maintaining aerospace superiority over UEG worlds. For this purpose, the Air Force organizes, trains, and equips air and space forces to interdict and destroy enemy attacks before and after they enter orbit. Collateral functions include:

○ Deployment and maintenance of UNSC unmanned defense satellites and orbital weapon platforms.

○ Monitoring and regulation of military and civilian orbital activities.

○ Development of doctrine, procedures, and equipment that are of common interest to the Army and Navy.

○ Furnishing launch and space support for the Army and Navy.

# UNSC RANKS

## OFFICERS

UNSC officers are commissioned, meaning that their authority is granted by a formal legal document issued on the authority of the UEG President. This commission is awarded after the completion of Officer Candidate School (OCS) and after taking the oath of service.

## WARRANT OFFICERS

Warrant officers are technical specialists and subject matter experts who are given an officer's commission in recognition of their expertise and leadership role. They take the officer's oath of service and are rated above enlisted troops, but are subordinate to full officers. The Air Force does not select or utilize warrant officers, and they are rarely found in the Marine Corps.

## NON-COMMISSIONED OFFICERS

Non-commissioned officers (NCOs) are enlisted personnel that fill most intermediary leadership and administrative roles, though their responsibilities vary by service, occupational specialty, and duty station. The UNSC relies heavily on its NCOs, and they share many responsibilities with officers.

## THORNE

Even though there are more than a few Master Chief Petty Officers, in the fleet we call them by the old nickname of "Top Chief" out of respect for John-117.

# NAVCOM RANKS

The Navy and ONI use rank titles which are different from the other branches of service. Navy ranks and terminology have a long, rich history that dates back many centuries, to an era where ships sailed on oceans of water and not between the stars.

While aboard Navy ships you will report to the ship captain in all matters related to the safety and security of the ship, superseding other responsibilities and orders. In all other cases, your Spartan Commander has operational control and you cannot be given, or give, orders to Navy or ONI personnel. Nevertheless, as a guest on the ship, be respectful and accommodate all reasonable requests that do not violate your orders or the Spartan Code.

| RANK | ABBREVIATION | TYPICAL RESPONSIBILITIES |
|---|---|---|
| CREWMAN RECRUIT | CR | BOOT CAMP AND TRAINING SCHOOL |
| CREWMAN APPRENTICE | CA | INITIAL FLEET ASSIGNMENT |
| CREWMAN | CR | WORK CREW |
| PETTY OFFICER THIRD CLASS | PO3 | WORK PARTY LEAD |
| PETTY OFFICER SECOND CLASS | PO2 | COMPARTMENT SUPERVISOR |
| PETTY OFFICER FIRST CLASS | PO1 | WORK DIVISION SUPERVISOR |
| CHIEF PETTY OFFICER | CPO | DECK SUPERVISOR |
| SENIOR CHIEF PETTY OFFICER | SCPO | OVERSIGHT OF SHIP ENLISTED PERSONNEL |
| MASTER CHIEF PETTY OFFICER | MCPO | FLEET ADMINISTRATION OR HIGHCOM STAFF |

## OFFICER RANKS

| RANK CODE | NAME | ABBREVIATION | TYPICAL RESPONSIBILITIES |
|---|---|---|---|
| OT | CADET | CDT | NO COMMAND AUTHORITY. |
| WO-1 | WARRANT OFFICER | WO | RESIDENT TECHNICAL EXPERT. |
| WO-2 | CHIEF WARRANT OFFICER | CWO | COMMAND ADVISOR OR CAPTAIN OF UTILITY SHIP. |
| O-1 | ENSIGN | ENS | INITIAL OFFICER POSTING. |
| O-2 | LIEUTENANT JUNIOR GRADE | LTJG | COMMAND OF STAFF SECTION. |
| O-3 | LIEUTENANT | LT | COMMAND OF WORK DIVISION OR CAPTAIN OF SUPPORT SHIP. |
| O-4 | LIEUTENANT COMMANDER | LCDR | FIRST OFFICER ON SMALL WARSHIP OR COMMAND OF SHIP DEPARTMENT. |
| O-5 | COMMANDER | CDR | HIGHCOM STAFF OR CAPTAIN OF SMALL WARSHIP. |
| O-6 | CAPTAIN | CAPT | CAPTAIN OF LINE WARSHIP OR INSTALLATION. |
| O-7 | REAR ADMIRAL | RADM | BATTLE GROUP COMMANDER. |
| O-8 | VICE ADMIRAL | VADM | COMMAND OF SECTOR FLEET OR ACADEMY. |
| O-9 | ADMIRAL | ADM | HIGHCOM STAFF. |
| O-10 | FLEET ADMIRAL | FADM | FLEET COMMANDER. |

# UNICOM RANKS

**THORNE**

"Master Guns" is the accepted nickname for a Master Gunnery Sergeant, and you'll often hear Master Sergeants called "Top" in the Army and Marine Corps.

The UNSC ground forces are a lean organization, with very little administrative overhead and bureaucracy. Artificial intelligences and automated services handle most routine paperwork and coordination, allowing the warfighters to concentrate on their military duties. The UNSC's exemplary standards of training and high "tooth to tail" ratio of fighting troops to support personnel also means that senior enlisted and junior officers are given far more responsibility and command authority than was historically possible.

## ENLISTED RANKS

| RANK CODE | NAME | ABBREVIATION | TYPICAL RESPONSIBILITIES |
|-----------|------|--------------|--------------------------|
| E-1 | PRIVATE | PVT | BOOT CAMP AND TRAINING SCHOOL. |
| E-2 | PRIVATE FIRST CLASS | PFC | INITIAL ASSIGNMENT. |
| E-3 | LANCE CORPORAL | LCPL | FIRETEAM ASSISTANT. |
| E-4 | CORPORAL | CPL | FIRETEAM LEADER. |
| E-5 | SERGEANT | SGT | SQUAD LEADER. |
| E-6 | STAFF SERGEANT | SSGT | ASSISTANT PLATOON LEADER. |
| E-7 | GUNNERY SERGEANT | GYSGT | ASSISTANT COMPANY COMMANDER. |
| E-8 | MASTER SERGEANT | MSGT | DIVISION ADMINISTRATION. E-8 TECHNICAL CAREER TRACK. |
| E-8 | FIRST SERGEANT | 1SGT | ASSISTANT BATTALION COMMANDER. E-8 COMMAND CAREER TRACK. |
| E-9 | MASTER GUNNERY SERGEANT | MGSGT | STAFF LEAD. E-9 TECHNICAL CAREER TRACK. |
| E-9 | SERGEANT MAJOR | SGTMAJ | ASSISTANT DIVISION COMMANDER. E-9 COMMAND CAREER TRACK. |

## OFFICER RANKS

| RANK CODE | NAME | ABBREVIATION | TYPICAL RESPONSIBILITIES |
|-----------|------|--------------|--------------------------|
| OT | CADET | CDT | NO COMMAND AUTHORITY. |
| WO-1 | WARRANT OFFICER | WO | CREW CHIEF OR ARMY PILOT. |
| WO-2 | CHIEF WARRANT OFFICER | CWO | SENIOR SUBJECT MATTER EXPERT. |
| O-1 | SECOND LIEUTENANT | 2LT | PLATOON COMMANDER. |
| O-2 | FIRST LIEUTENANT | 1LT | COMPANY EXECUTIVE OFFICER. |
| O-3 | CAPTAIN | CPT | COMPANY COMMANDER. |
| O-4 | MAJOR | MAJ | BATTALION EXECUTIVE OFFICER. |
| O-5 | LIEUTENANT COLONEL | LTCOL | BATTALION COMMANDER. |
| O-6 | COLONEL | COL | BRIGADE COMMANDER. |
| O-7 | BRIGADIER GENERAL | BGEN | DIVISION COMMANDER. |
| O-8 | MAJOR GENERAL | MGEN | TASK FORCE COMMANDER. |
| O-9 | LIEUTENANT GENERAL | LTGEN | CENTCOM COMMANDER. |
| O-10 | GENERAL | GEN | HIGHCOM SENIOR STAFF. |

# PART 09

# ALIEN FACTIONS

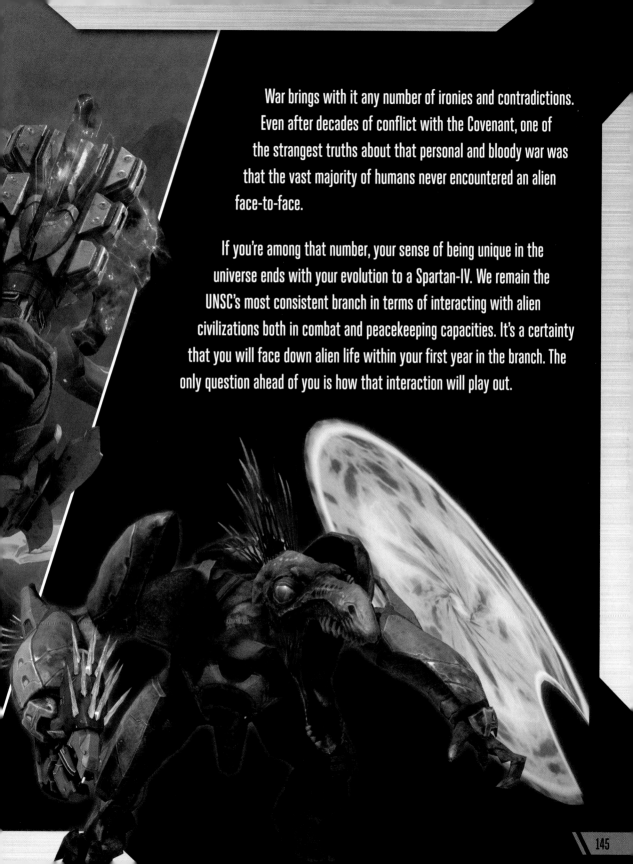

War brings with it any number of ironies and contradictions. Even after decades of conflict with the Covenant, one of the strangest truths about that personal and bloody war was that the vast majority of humans never encountered an alien face-to-face.

If you're among that number, your sense of being unique in the universe ends with your evolution to a Spartan-IV. We remain the UNSC's most consistent branch in terms of interacting with alien civilizations both in combat and peacekeeping capacities. It's a certainty that you will face down alien life within your first year in the branch. The only question ahead of you is how that interaction will play out.

# SANGHEILI (ELITES)

When humanity first encountered this proud warrior race, we gave them the name Elites, and perhaps no term better signifies what the Sangheili are. During the Covenant War, Sangheili were our most challenging and dangerous enemy combatants. But even before the final days of the conflict, where a majority of their people realized the error of blindly following the Covenant leadership, a grudging respect existed between our two peoples.

Separated from the authority of the San'Shyuum Prophets for the first time in thousands of years, most Elites have return to rebuild their homeworlds and reestablish themselves as an independent and moderate force in the galaxy. However, the civil war that's broken out among Sangheili factions aligned with remnants of the Covenant and the Arbiter now jeopardizes that hard-fought peace.

# SANGHEILI

## THREAT LEVEL: HIGH

*MACTO COGNATUS*

HOMEWORLD: SANGHELIOS

HEIGHT RANGE: 2230–2590 MM (7 FT 4IN–8 FT 6IN)

WEIGHT RANGE: 139–178 KG (307–393 LB)

Sangheili are biped saurians with tall, muscular bodies. Their bodies are covered entirely in fine, leathery scales, with elongated serpentine heads with four mandibles, the upper and lower of which are each lined with sharp rows of teeth. Sangheili can splay open their mandibles but tend to keep them closed, especially when communicating. Sangheili have long, sinewy arms that end in zygodactyl hands, bearing long but dexterous clawed fingers (two thumbs and twin forefingers). Their legs are digitigrade and well suited for long-distance running.

Younger Sangheili have pale protective scales around their necks, believed to be vestigial and from a time when offspring were carried by the neck. The color of scales (shades of brown, gray, and black), structure of mandibles, and teeth count vary between population groups, evidence of significant genetic drift between colonies over their thousands of years of interstellar civilization. Their faces have twin nostril slits just below their eyes, and Sangheili have a sense of smell far more refined than humans. Sangheili sight is roughly human-equivalent both in the spectra they perceive and depth perception.

## TACTICAL NOTES

All Sangheili are trained from an early age to engage in hand-to-hand combat and use both close-range and long-range weaponry, both archaic and plasma-based. Advancement in the military is hinged on individual and personal merit, generally measured in the amount of kills one as secured. Though crude, this rubric has proven remarkably effective.

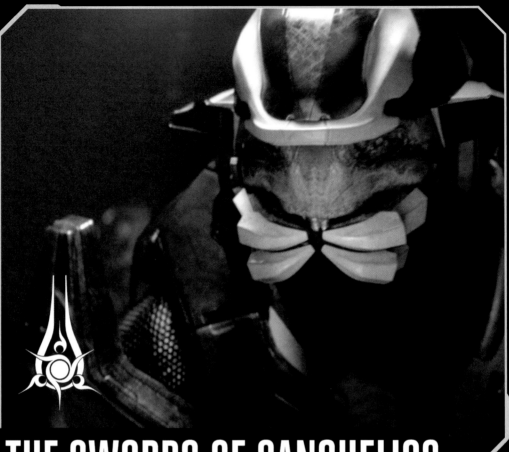

# THE SWORDS OF SANGHELIOS

As the UNSC has seen firsthand, no Sangheili is more honorable nor braver than the former Supreme Commander named named Thel 'Vadam. Yet the being known as the Arbiter (a warrior-king title from deep in Sangheili tradition) has always been an unlikely foe of the religious fundamentalism that led his people astray. A dedicated yet quiet soldier whose faith was shaken at the end of the war, 'Vadam has found himself in a position to lead where no one else will. That contradiction gave birth to the Swords of Sanghelios.

Naming themselves for a warrior band from their culture's mythic past, the Swords are a brotherhood dedicated to the preservation of a unified Sangheili people. In that way, comparisons with our own Spartan ranks are not unwelcome. But many Elites are still held in the sway of old beliefs about the Covenant, and there are many who would exploit those tensions in their own quest for power.

# THE COVENANT

Chief among the forces fighting against the Swords of Sanghelios is an alliance of warlords and zealots led by a brilliant commander who has forged many Covenant remnant fleets and colonies into an empire. Having gathered warriors discontent with the truce brokered between the Arbiter and humanity, 'Mdama declared himself the head of a new Covenant dedicated to erasing both the Swords of Sanghelios and the UNSC from the galaxy. 'Mdama's heavily armed faction of represents a significant threat to the fragile peace that Thel 'Vadam has brought to both our peoples.

[R5]

[R5]

[R2]

[R3]

[R7]

[R6]

[R4]

# THEL 'VADAM

## THE ARBITER

HEIGHT: 2386 MM (7 FT 10 IN)
WEIGHT: 144.7 KG (319 LB)
BIRTHWORLD: SANGHELIOS

The Arbiter was once a devoted Covenant warrior, before being betrayed by the Prophet of Truth and discovering the Covenant's belief system was based on misinterpretations and lies. He forged a fragile alliance with the Master Chief and led a band of rebel Sangheili against the Covenant during the Great Schism, helping crush his former allies and bring an end to the war.

Returning home to Sanghelios he took control of his family's keep and took on the Arbiter's ancient responsibility of leader and peacemaker. Those who follow the Arbiter do so with the utmost of loyalty, although his enemies are many and power struggles on Sanghelios have weakened his armies. Undaunted even as the Covenant makes its push on Sanghelios, the Arbiter sees the opportunity to crush his enemies arrayed in open battle and end the civil strife on his world once and for all.

## IDENTIFICATION

Thel 'Vadam retains possession of the Arbiter combat harness he used when fighting alongside the Master Chief, though in his day-to-day tasks as leader of the Swords of Sanghelios he wears ceremonial plate that marks him as a Kaidon ("lord") of Vadam Keep.

[R5]
[R5]
[R2]
[R3]
[R7]
[R6]

[R4]

# JUL 'MDAMA

## THE HAND OF THE DIDACT

HEIGHT: 2399 MM (7 FT 10 IN)
WEIGHT: 148.3 KG (327 LB)
BIRTHWORLD: SANGHELIOS

Jul 'Mdama was once a loyal commander within the old Covenant, but his discontent with the Arbiter and imprisonment by ONI made him obsessive and vengeful. After locating the Didact, he pledged his loyalty to the awakened Forerunner general and received his blessing to command his constructs. With the apparent defeat of the Didact, this now places Jul 'Mdama at the head of a large host of mechanized warriors, in addition to giving him considerable influence in the Covenant due to the Forerunner's blessing.

## IDENTIFICATION

'Mdama wears black Zealot armor decorated with the symbol for the Hand of the Didact. His helmet bears a holographic Forerunner glyph of unknown meaning.

# SANGHEILI THREATS

Divisions within Sangheili culture are almost innumerable, ranging from the level of manor lords and elders, to artisan-armorer and farmer. The ranks of the warrior are the most important for Spartans to be familiar with, particularly the divisions found within the Covenant.

## ELITE MINOR \\ STORM ELITE

### ROLE: HEAVY INFANTRY

Usually clad in blue armor, Minors are the lowest of Sangheili ranks within the Covenant. Despite their lower rank, Elite Minors are strong and formidable warriors, capable of leading other species in tactical groups known as lances (roughly equivalent to a UNSC squad). Within Jul 'Mdama's Covenant, these Sangheili warriors are classified as Storm Elites, which was previously reserved for Sangheili in more prestigious shock-trooper roles.

## ELITE ULTRA

### ROLE: STRIKE TEAMS

The highest of standard infantry is the Elite Ultra classification, generally clad in white armor. Also known as the Evocati, Ultras can be utilized as effective leaders, commanding Elite Majors and Minors alike, but they are also proficient at operating and functioning as lone wolves in the field.

## ELITE SPECOPS

### ROLE: SPECIAL FORCES

Very little is known about the groups of Sangheili that ONI designates as Special Operations Elites, beyond the fact that they are the most proficient tactical unit within the Covenant military. These highly trained and unusually subtle Elites are rarely encountered in the field, and all encounters should be immediately logged with HighCom.

# ELITE ZEALOT

### ROLE: DOCTRINAL ENFORCEMENT

Less of a rank than a philosophy of commitment and combat, Zealots are by far the most ruthless and uncompromising warriors within all the Covenant military. Loyal only to the tenets of the Covenant and the dogma of their specific warrior-monastery order, the Zealots take to the field as independent combat forces clad in gold red-violet armor, ready to judge the unworthy at the point of an energy sword.

# ELITE MAJOR

### ROLE: LOW COMMAND

A slightly higher command role than the Minor and oftentimes leading a squad of fellow Sangheili, the Elite Major role (formally referred to as an Obedientiary) features better weapons and armor, but only marginally so. Usually clad in red armor.

# ELITE GENERAL

### ROLE: HIGH COMMAND

Elite Generals command legions of Covenant warriors, managing ground operations when the direct occupation of an enemy's territory is necessary. During some campaigns, multiple Generals are required, each working in concert with the others to effectively cover the theater of war. Generals typically wear elaborately decorated gold armor in battle.

# JIRALHANAE (BRUTES)

A towering and muscular species that UNSC troops called the Brutes, Jiralhanae culture is defined by survival of the strongest, and a bitter sense of competition runs through everything they do. In the centuries before the Covenant discovered the Brutes, the species had nearly destroyed their own planet in a massive nuclear conflict, the scars of which remain even today. But Brutes tend to thrive where the environment is harshest, and that tenacity is what makes them such a dangerous foe.

Without the guidance of the Prophets or the powerful chieftains that served them, the Jiralhanae have once again broken into competing clans bound by ties of blood, oath, and mutual interest. Intermittent warfare continues on Doisac and other Brute territories between alliances fighting for access to the remaining Covenant ships and resources, though all are loosely united against non-Jiralhanae interference.

[R5]
[R5]
[R2]
[R3]
[R7]
[R6]
[R4]

# JIRALHANAE

## THREAT LEVEL: VERY HIGH

*SERVUS FEROX*
HOMEWORLD: DOISAC
HEIGHT RANGE: 2590–2800 MM (8 FT 5 IN–9 FT 2 IN)
WEIGHT RANGE: 500–680 KG (1,125–1500 LB)

Averaging nearly three meters in height, the Jiralhanae are an aggressive species of pseudo-ursine mammalian bipeds. Without any grooming, Jiralhanae will become completely covered in thick brown or black fur, which whitens as they age. Beneath their fur is a tough, leathery gray skin, similar in texture to that of an African black rhino. They have three clawed fingers and an opposable thumb on each hand, with large cloven-toed feet. Their sense of smell is exceptional, though sight and hearing are within human norms. Jiralhanae are omnivorous, but their sharp teeth and high caloric requirements betray a mostly carnivorous diet.

## TACTICAL NOTES

Jiralhanae society values strength and ferocity above all, though cunning and stealth is also highly prized. The basic unit of social cohesion is the pack, consisting of families or military squads led by a dominant alpha male; Jiralhanae who reject the pack structure are considered deviants of the highest order.

# THE BANISHED

The Banished are an alliance of privateers and raiders unified under the banner of a powerful Jiralhanae warlord named Atriox. While many Jiralhanae chieftains are suspicious of, or outright hostile to, any other race, this army of former Covenant warriors has invited a range of deadly allies to their cause. Atriox has displayed a knack for building alliances and machines of war, and a talent for locating the richest targets to raid.

Atriox is reported to have led a fleet of Banished to an unknown destination, but the chieftains he has organized and controlled continue to spread their influence and power throughout Brute colonies and even into human criminal enterprises. ONI is still researching what Atriox and the Banished ultimately hope to achieve, but Spartans should be on high alert that future encounters with Brutes and other raiders will likely show far more direction and strategy than has previously been the case.

**THORNE**

This is what I signed up for —not just a chance to fight, but a chance to beat back some of the ugliest bullies in the universe.

[R5]
[R5]
[R2]
[R3]
[R7]
[R6]

[R4]

# ATRIOX

## WARMASTER OF THE BANISHED

HEIGHT: 2603 MM (8 FT 6 IN)
WEIGHT: 635 KG (1400 LB)
BIRTHWORLD: DOISAC

Leader and creator of the Banished, Atriox is a fearsome warrior who rose to power by his charismatic personality and talent for shrewd strategic planning honed during the Covenant War. As one of the few heretics who survived—even prospered—after his rebellion early in the war, Atriox has accumulated an impressive reputation among former Covenant forces. With a cunning that is uncharacteristic of most Brute chieftains, Atriox has skillfully exploited his legend to build a larger-than-life persona that attracts malcontents from every species.

## IDENTIFICATION

Atriox wears a custom suit of Jiralhanae battleplate and is almost never without his favored energy mace, "Chainbreaker," within reach. Be aware that Atriox has displayed top-tier combat abilities, and Spartans are not advised to engage except in joint operations.

---

**GRANT**

Atriox . . . haven't even met him, and I already don't like him.

158

[R5]

[R5]

[R2]

[R3]

[R7]

[R6]

[R4]

# DECIMUS

## BANISHED WAR CHIEFTAIN
HEIGHT: 2800 MM (9 FT 3 IN)
WEIGHT: 680.4 KG (1500 LB)
BIRTHWORLD: DOISAC

Decimus is the embodiment of every horror story UNSC soldiers swap about fighting the Brutes. He's ruthless, gloriously bloodthirsty, and almost unparalleled in raw physical strength. He takes particular delight in hand-to-hand combat with woefully outmatched opponents, shattering their resolve with unstoppable berserker fury. He serves as one of Atriox's most trusted field commanders, and has served as the Banished second-in-command for years.

## IDENTIFICATION
Decimus wears a suit of Jiralhanae battleplate in most situations, but in the field he has also been recorded using an exoframe of unknown origin to further enhance his already impressive strength.

# JIRALHANAE THREATS

Warlike and violent, Brutes were the first Banished, and they form the bulk of Atriox's ground forces. Banished Brutes naturally organize into packs, with alphas and chieftains rising up to lead through physical force and proven ability.

## BRUTE MINORS
### ROLE: HEAVY INFANTRY

Many Brutes in the service of the Banished are placed in charge of allied forces that require a stern hand and constant supervision to keep them focused on the mission (notably, Grunts). These groups echo much of the discipline exhibited by Brutes late in the Covenant War, which is a stark contrast to the near-feral aggression exhibited by most independent Jiralhanae groups.

## BRUTE CAPTAINS
### ROLE: LOW COMMAND

Brute Captains within the Banished lead the terror and raiding packs that extort resources and smash the defenses of the settlements they raid. They also lead attacks on Doisac itself, impressing independent clans with their strength and killing rival warlords who refuse to bow to Atriox.

## BRUTE CHIEFTAINS
### ROLE: SPECIAL FORCES

Brute Chieftains are high-ranking Jiralhanae pack commanders, identifiable by their striking red-and-black armor and ornate headdresses. Their armor features embedded shield generators, which offers a considerable amount of protection.

# BANISHED ALLIES ///////////////

The Banished are a multi-species alliance bound by the will of Atriox and a hunger for profit and power. In theory, all who can aid Atriox's ambition and will bend the knee are welcome, from human to Hunter, but their violence and conditions of service limit recruitment opportunities.

## BANISHED ELITES

Strong and proud, with a refined martial tradition, the Elites in service of the Banished are primarily mercenaries paid in resources and military equipment needed for inter-clan and factional warfare back in their home colonies.

## BANISHED GRUNTS

Grunts are a fast-breeding species of methane-breathing bipeds used by the Banished as disposable laborers and soldiers. Most Unggoy in the service of the Banished were culled from Covenant breeding colonies or acquired during raids and serve without much enthusiasm, despite the motivating violence of their Brute overseers.

## BANISHED HUNTERS

The loyalties and goals of the Lekgolo colonies working for the Banished are unknown. ONI has noted unusual deviations from previously established behavior patterns for the Hunters in Banished service, and Spartans are ordered to observe and report on Banished Hunter activities rather than engage, if possible.

## PROMETHEANS

Although the original Forerunner Prometheans were flesh-and-blood warriors, in the final days of the Forerunner-Flood War, the last of their numbers submitted themselves to Composition—a destructive process that turned their minds into digital essences, which were immune to the corruption of the parasite when encased in mechanized Knight constructs. These Promethean Knights were later augmented by Composed humans, impressed into battle by their general, the Didact. It remains unknown how many—if any—Forerunner essences remain in the Knight legions encountered at Requiem and Oban.

[R5]
[R5]
[R2]
[R3]
[R7]
[R6]

[R4]

# KNIGHTS

## THREAT LEVEL: VERY HIGH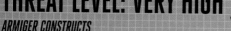

*ARMIGER CONSTRUCTS*

HOMEWORLD: REQUIEM
HEIGHT RANGE: 3023–3677 MM (9 FT 11 IN–12 FT 2 IN)
WEIGHT RANGE: 407.3–423.7 KG (898–934 LB)

Knights exhibit height and mass variance even between otherwise identical bodies, though the significance of this is unknown. Their bodies are humanoid, with distinctive insectoid characteristics, and are bound together with hard light and force field linkages rather than mechanical servos. They have two pairs of arms, though their smaller arms appear to be a vestige or design flaw, and are nonfunctional. Their heads are armored, and most encase what appears to be a glowing human skull, which is revealed during attacks—presumably as an intimidation tactic. It is unclear if this can be used to distinguish between Knights that possess human or Forerunner essences.

With the disappearance of the Didact, Knight forces under the command of Jul 'Mdama have begun to rapidly change, and Knights that have recently been encountered among the Covenant forces now show substantial design differences in both shape and coloration. This is an unexpected development, and acquiring intact Knight mechanisms is a high-priority task from ONI.

[R5]
[R5]
[R2]
[R3]
[R7]
[R6]

### GRANT

Wait, the additional records you sent me say that this guy was a . . . political prisoner? How does that work? Why? Who put him in Requiem? Why did he have it out for humanity the second he was released?

### THORNE

His wife put him there. Look, it's a long story. Ask Halsey about it the next time you see her.

# THE DIDACT

## PROTECTOR OF ECUMENE

HEIGHT: 3454 MM (11 FT 4 IN)
WEIGHT: 360.6 KG (794.9 LB)

An ancient Forerunner commander, the Didact was once the victim of a political conflict with another sect of Forerunners. Forced into exile within the shield world of Requiem in the final days of the Forerunner-Flood War, he was awakened a hundred millennia later and led an attack on Earth. Although seemingly defeated, ONI remains vigilant.

## IDENTIFICATION

The Didact wears a distinctive suit of Forerunner battle armor that is unique to him. Any sightings of the Didact are to be reported to ONI immediately.

# PROMETHEAN THREATS ///////////////

The Prometheans, or more accurately, the Knight constructs who serve in their name, are but one class of war machine that was created and used by the Didact.

## KNIGHTS

### ROLE: HEAVY INFANTRY

The Knights are purpose-built to combat the parasitic Flood, and are armed with a variety of weapon systems, which are well suited for dealing with biological threats. Unfortunately, this also makes their weapons and tactics quite useful against the UNSC, and in recent weeks since the destruction of Requiem, their behavior patterns have also begun to show signs of optimizing against both Spartan and Covenant attack patterns.

## CRAWLERS

### ROLE: LIGHT INFANTRY

Mass-produced in nanotech assembler vats on Requiem, the quadruped Crawlers are expendable robotic infantry deployed in large numbers to assist the Knights in their duties. Fast and able to climb sheer surfaces, the Crawlers are incredibly mobile and capable of infiltrating spaces that conventional troops would find impossible to traverse.

## WATCHERS

### ROLE: SUPPORT

The Watchers are support constructs, which aid the Knights in battle with a variety of energy projectors and defensive weapons. Each Knight carries a Watcher for direct support, and they should be considered priority targets due to their ability to rapidly reform Knight construct bodies.

# SAN'SHYUUM (PROPHETS)

The former lords of the Covenant, the San'Shyuum who survived the war have fled to parts unknown, pursued by vengeful Sangheili and the UNSC. ONI and the Swords of Sanghelios continue to work to locate the destination of the Prophet war criminals and bring them to justice.

## THREAT LEVEL: LOW

*PERFIDIA VERMIS*
HOMEWORLD: JANJUR QOM
HEIGHT RANGE: 2134–2261 MM (7 FT–7 FT 5 IN)
WEIGHT RANGE: 81.4–96.6 KG (179.4–212.9 LB)

### THORNE

I don't know a single Spartan who has seen so much as a wrinkly wattle of these guys in over five years. With any luck they met a bad end during their escape out of the Orion Arm. Good riddance.

Contemporary San'Shyuum are tall, lithe creatures with long serpentine necks and thin, frail skeletal structures, which require slow and delicate movement. They are tridactyl fingered with narrow, highly tactile hands and prehensile (though often atrophied to a point of uselessness) feet. While younger San'Shyuum still walk upright like their ancestors, many adults and elders, particularly those in places of authority, now utilize anti-gravity systems for mobility. Despite their physical impediments, the San'Shyuum have been able to dramatically extended their lifespans through medical advancements, allowing many individuals to live for hundreds of years.

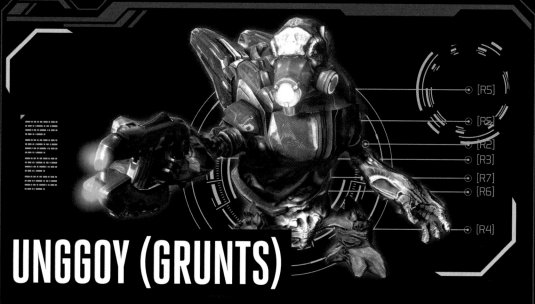

[R5]
[R5]
[R2]
[R3]
[R7]
[R6]
[R4]

# UNGGOY (GRUNTS)

As the UNSC's name for these aliens implies, the Covenant used the Unggoy as disposal foot soldiers and laborers. Unggoy are not naturally aggressive, but centuries of oppression and subservience means that many are still in service to warlords of various stripes.

## THREAT LEVEL: VERY LOW.
## HIGH WHEN IN LARGE GROUPS

*MONACHUS FRIGUS*
HOMEWORLD: BALAHO
HEIGHT RANGE: 1384–1670 MM (4 FT 6 IN–5 FT 7 IN)
WEIGHT RANGE: 112.6–118 KG (248.3–260.1 LB)

### THORNE

Take note of their size, Spartan. Civilians and even many new UNSC recruits think Grunts are comical little guys with squeaky voices (and they are), but they're also much bigger than you think, and strong enough to tear your arm off if they get angry.

Unggoy are squat, xenoarthropodal bipeds who appear to have originated from smaller amphibious primate analogues in the methane-rich water bodies of their home planet. Their bodies are compact and reminiscent of crustaceans, despite being vertebrates. Distinct from many other bipeds, Unggoy hind legs are quite short, designed more for clambering and crawling over rocky terrain than walking upright. Their disproportionately large arms are excellent for grappling and scaling, but often impede attempts to move through narrow corridors or manipulate small, delicate objects. Large portions of their backs, arms, and legs are covered in rigid exoskeleton, lined with barbs and spikes, though the extent of this coverage varies within type. Unggoy have bright blue blood, a bioluminescence attributed to their methane-based respiratory system.

[R5]
[R5]
[R2]
[R3]
[R7]
[R6]

[R4]

# KIG-YAR (JACKALS)

Always waiting on the edge of an alien battle, the quick killers known as Kig-Yar don't like fighting in an open field—they prefer stealth. A mercenary species through and through, it's a certainty that Kig-Yar are out there looking for contracts both for and against human interests.

## THREAT LEVEL: MEDIUM

### PEROSUS LATRUNCULUS
HOMEWORLD: EAYN
HEIGHT RANGE: 1900–2030 MM (6 FT 2 IN–6 FT 8 IN)
WEIGHT RANGE: 88–93 KG (194–205 LB)

### THORNE

The interiors of Kig-Yar ships smell like . . . lavender. ONI folks say it's some sort of therapeutic chemical they pump into the air supply.

Kig-Yar are a highly evolved saurian species with distinct avian attributes, having developed into swift bipedal omnivores with nimble bodies that are lissome and designed for tracking prey. Kig-Yar have strong legs with three-toed feet and can reach speeds of up to 72 km/h (45 mph) in open areas, due to their lightweight bone structure and very powerful musculature. Their torso is lean, with low shoulders and long, slender arms, which end in tri-digit hands, easily capable of gripping and manipulating tools, machines, and weapons. Kig-Yar center of gravity is low to the ground, allowing for quick tactical changes to direction, aided by three large claws on both hands and feet. Their blood is a bright violet color.

### GRANT

Uh. Thanks for the info?

[R5]
[R5]
[R2]
[R3]
[R7]
[R6]

[R4]

# MGALEKGOLO (HUNTERS)

The first time you encounter a Hunter in the field, remind yourself that this is no tank. In fact, Mgalekgolo are actually colonies of eel-like creatures bound together and sharing a consciousness. The Mgalekgolo are an enigmatic species and can be friend or foe depending on who they have decided to ally themselves with.

## THREAT LEVEL: HIGH ⚠

*OPHIS CONGREGATIO*

HOMEWORLD: TE
HEIGHT RANGE: 3687–3734 MM (12FT 1 IN–12 FT 3 IN)
WEIGHT RANGE: 4536–4990 KG (10000–11000 LB)

Mgalekgolo are tightly bound colonies consisting of dozens of individual Lekgolo "eels." In general, individual Lekgolo "eels" are 134 to 155 cm (52.8 to 61 in) long, though they vary dramatically in girth from 41 to 165 mm (1.6 to 6.5 in) and in mass between 5.6 to 30.7 kg (12.3 to 67.7 lb) each. An individual Lekgolo is typically one of several shades of orange, segmented along the length of the creature. Its blood is a luminously bright orange with a dense, muddy texture. Individual Lekgolo possess animallike cognitive abilities, but their intelligence scales rapidly in large groups. The Covenant provided armored Hunter frames for the Mgalekgolo gestalts, equipped with sensors, which offered enhanced "sight" and a massive fuel rod cannon for offensive use. Other Lekgolo gestalt types are used to control large vehicles, such as the Scarab, proving that the species is highly adaptable.

[R4]

# YANME'E (DRONES)

The Yanme'e are a hive-like species organized around their Queens. The Drones have rarely presented a threat to the UNSC since the fall of the Covenant, though it seems the secrets of easily communicating with this species was lost with the disappearance of the Prophets. Individual Drones possess limited intelligence and agency, but when organized by a Queen they can exhibit extremely complicated behaviors.

## THREAT LEVEL: LOW

*TURPIS REX*
HOMEWORLD: PALAMOK
HEIGHT RANGE: 1778–2058 MM (5FT 10 IN-6 FT 9 IN)
WEIGHT RANGE: 77–127 KG (169.7–280 LB)

The Yanme'e are omniverous arthropods that have evolved into sentient beings capable of limited flight. Anatomically, they are bipedal insectoids with chitinous exoskeletons and two pairs of wings. Yanme'e are poly-dextrous, capable of using both their hands and prehensile feet to grasp tools, weapons, and even enemies while in combat. Yanme'e blood displays a range of bioluminescent colors, which varies based on their diet.

Communication between individual Yanme'e occurs both sonically and by way of pheromones, making communication with other species challenging. Most Yanme'e fall into one of three distinct castes: domestic, worker, or protector, although the Covenant artificially merged the latter two. To outsiders, males and females look extremely similar, though small changes in coloration or silhouette can indicate class and function. Yanme'e Queens are substantially larger than the rest in their species with distended abdomens and thick legs.

# HURAGOK (ENGINEERS)

The Huragok are actually biological machines created by the Forerunners to maintain their various installations and technologies. Engineers have an intuitive knowledge of all technology. When humanity first encountered these Engineers during the war, we saw them dismantle, reassemble, and ultimately improve some of our best technology in moments. In recent years, humanity has learned much about the Huragok, though all but a few were killed in the final days of the Covenant. Locating, acquiring, and protecting these creatures is an extremely vital mission typically assigned exclusively to Spartans.

## THREAT LEVEL: NONE

*FACTICIUS INDOLES*
HOMEWORLD: N/A
HEIGHT RANGE: 1800–2480 MM (5 FT 11 IN–8 FT 2 IN)
WEIGHT RANGE: 56–57 KG (123–126 LB)

The Huragok are approximately the size of an average human male, though their mode of locomotion is vastly different. Huragok float above the ground, lifted by lighter-than-air gases stored in bladders on their backs. Huragok normally float a few feet above the ground, although in special situations they are able to rise much higher for short periods of time. Despite possessing no true tissues or organs, the nanochemical surrogates closely mimic biological structures to all but the most in-depth examination.

# THE FLOOD

## THREAT LEVEL: EXTREME (OMEGA) ⚠

The Flood is a voracious hive-mind omni-parasite capable of seizing, converting, and controlling sentient hosts. Infected individuals have their nervous systems hijacked by the parasite, turning their bodies into puppets while their memories are exploited to further the infestation.

## ///////////////// ☣ WARNING! BIOHAZARD ☣ /////////////////

There is no cure or treatment for Flood infection; infected creatures are to be killed on sight and their remains cremated, if possible. Spartans are expressively prohibited to gather biological samples or attempt treatment of infected individuals. UPSILON containment protocols are **ALWAYS** active when Flood presence is suspected, and any deviation from these measures is punishable in the harshest possible terms.

## EMERGENCY CONTACT PROTOCOL UPSILON

Immediately move to limit Flood expansion and initiate full quarantine. All UEG and UNSC rules of engagement are suspended for duration of containment efforts.

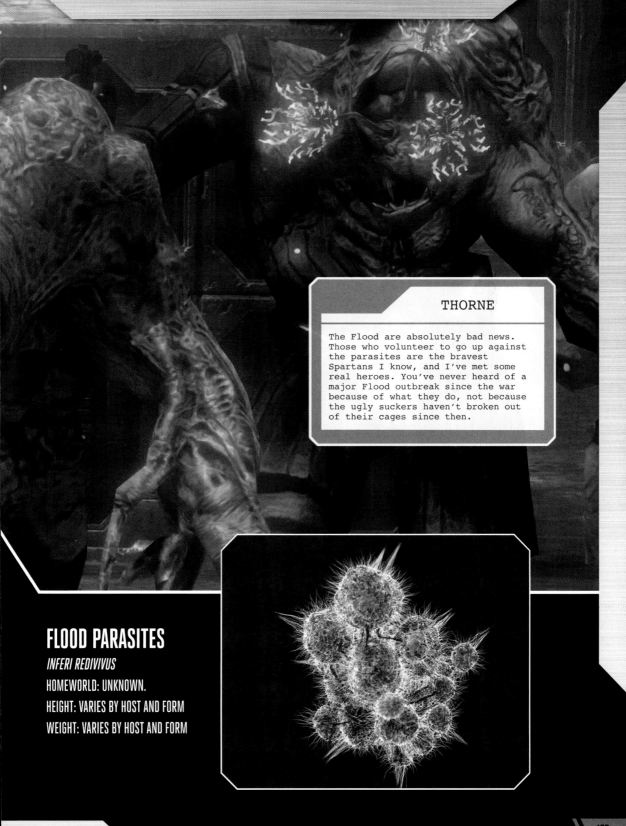

# FLOOD PARASITES

*INFERI REDIVIVUS*

HOMEWORLD: UNKNOWN.

HEIGHT: VARIES BY HOST AND FORM

WEIGHT: VARIES BY HOST AND FORM

# FLOOD THREATS  //////////////

The Flood are capable of infecting any living creature, though they have demonstrated a preference for targeting sapient creatures above all others. Infected individuals are forced to share all they know with the parasite, including the plans of allies, passcodes, and other secrets. Information compartmentalization is of extreme importance in dealing with a Flood outbreak.

## INFECTION FORM

Flood infection forms are nightmarish creatures spawned for the singular purpose of converting all thinking creatures into carriers, tools, and food for the parasite. They move quickly, adhering to virtually any surface with their tentacle-feet and leaping at any potential host.

## CARRIER FORM

Damaged combat forms and infected creatures who have outlived their usefulness are transformed into mobile incubation chambers for new Infection Forms. These bloated creatures attempt to close in and explosively release their parasite cargo. Engage at long range, if possible.

## COMBAT FORM

Creatures infested by an Infection Form are mutated into Flood killing machines that do not feel pain and have enhanced physical capabilities. Targeted shots against the limbs and the embedded Infection Form is an effective tactic. Combat Forms can use any equipment that their host knew how to operate.

## PURE FORMS

Encountering Pure Forms indicates an advanced stage of infestation. As these creatures can transition between various forms, it is recommended that heavy weapons be used immediately to prevent their adaptation to your weapons and tactics.

## BLIGHTLANDS

The region around Flood hives are twisted to serve the growth and expansion of the parasite, and all life in such an area is to be viewed as a hostile combatant. Thermobarics and incendiary weapons are recommended for tactical containment, but large outbreaks can only be cleansed with sustained plasma bombardment.

# /////////////// WARNING! ///////////////
# DECLARATION OF CRYPTONYM "CORRUPTER"

Declaration of the cryptonym CORRUPTER on the battlenet indicates that a Spartan has been infected by the Flood, safeguards failed, and weapons of mass destruction have been authorized for immediate release. All Spartans not assigned to Flood containment Fireteams are ordered to immediately activate emergency biohazard response UPSILON and withdraw to security perimeter. CORRUPTER protocol dictates containment and immediate bombardment with orbital MAC strikes and fusion warheads; evacuation may not be possible in some situations.

///////////////  WARNING! BIOHAZARD  ///////////////

# PART 10

UNSC
UNITED NATIONS SPACE COMMAND

# SPARTAN

# ARMORY

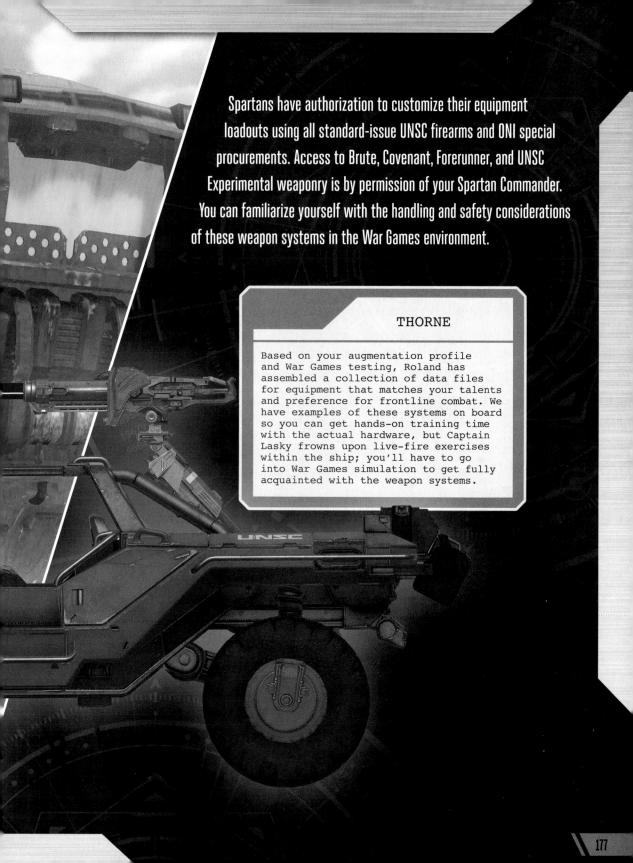

Spartans have authorization to customize their equipment loadouts using all standard-issue UNSC firearms and ONI special procurements. Access to Brute, Covenant, Forerunner, and UNSC Experimental weaponry is by permission of your Spartan Commander. You can familiarize yourself with the handling and safety considerations of these weapon systems in the War Games environment.

## THORNE

Based on your augmentation profile and War Games testing, Roland has assembled a collection of data files for equipment that matches your talents and preference for frontline combat. We have examples of these systems on board so you can get hands-on training time with the actual hardware, but Captain Lasky frowns upon live-fire exercises within the ship; you'll have to go into War Games simulation to get fully acquainted with the weapon systems.

# MJOLNIR POWERED ASSAULT ARMOR

The brainchild of Dr. Catherine Halsey, Project: MJOLNIR is a revolutionary powered armor system first envisioned as the counterpart to the Spartan human engineering program. Mjolnir armor enhances the combat abilities of Spartan super-soldiers far beyond what their base physiological augmentations are capable of. Throughout its decades of development and refinement Mjolnir became a symbol of humanity's ingenuity, adaptability, and fortitude in the face of impossible odds.

## ARMOR GENERATIONS

At its core, Mjolnir is a highly specialized weapon system, utilized exclusively by Spartan super-soldiers to engage enemy threats of various kinds. Initially this product focused on threats stemming from the Insurrection—its early functionality was limited to offensive and defensive combat modification against humans and human weapons. As the product advanced and improved over the years, other features were added to the Mjolnir platform, especially with regard to its functionality against Covenant technology, including a focus on defensive measures against directed energy weapons. After the war, a widespread privatization of the Mjolnir technology standards in 2553, coupled with a leveraging of Covenant technology and new developments borne out of Forerunner discoveries, skyrocketed Mjolnir technology into new areas of improvement and cost reduction, further increasing its combat abilities.

## GENERATION 1 MJOLNIR

All GEN1 Mjolnir suits are based on a unitary exoskeleton design, and do not have a techsuit. Although it is easy to dismiss early Mjolnir as outdated, the reality is that its disadvantages are due to the complexity of integrating its constantly evolving prototype technology with the ever-increasing capabilities of the Spartans themselves. This complexity led to massive costs, and a single Generation 1 suit is often benchmarked as equivalent to manufacturing a cruiser in terms of technical production needs and strategic resources expended in its creation and maintenance.

## GENERATION 2 MJOLNIR

GEN2 Mjolnir incorporated radical simplification of the overall exoskeleton architecture, reducing the number of complex components by an order of magnitude and bringing suits down in cost to the point that they could be mass-produced. Most of the suit's custom components were replaced by modular systems, sacrificing efficiency for large gains in ease of manufacture. Although a flexible platform, some in Spartan branch are dissatisfied with its minimal performance improvement over decades-old GEN1 systems.

# GENERATION 3 MJOLNIR

GEN3 is a conceptual design framework for next-generation Mjolnir, incorporating lessons learned from Generation 2 improvements while also returning to some of the performance characteristics and higher levels of protection offered by GEN1. The latest Mark VII armor iteration is the testbed for these improvements, though it remains to be seen if the major arms manufacturers are able to adopt this standard and still meet the rigorous cost accounting demanded by the UEG.

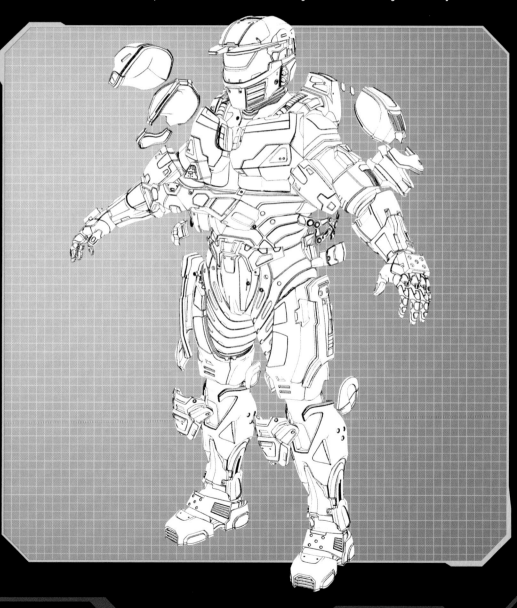

# MJOLNIR POWERED
# ASSAULT ARMOR ///////////////

## EARLY EXPERIMENTS

Later reclassified as the Mark I, Mark II, and Mark III by Dr. Catherine Halsey, ONI's early work with high-power exoskeleton systems was refined and greatly expanded upon during her development of Project: MJOLNIR.

## MARK I

While other exoskeleton efforts had come in the decades that preceded this line, Mark I was the first major endeavor of the Office of Naval Intelligence into robotic exoskeleton augmentation technology, as they had hoped to use it to enhance early super-soldier efforts like ORION. Over forty Mark I powered armor suits were manufactured, but none were fielded in battle due to a variety of limitations. The project was considered technically interesting but ultimately was canceled. Most Mark I suits were stored in classified material bunkers beneath the mountains of Reach.

## MARK II

The Mark II was a lighter and far more mobile variation of the Mark I, but it relied on a tether for power during development, as production of combat fusion generators proved to be far more difficult than originally estimated. The tether made it impractical for use in the field, though a number of these suits were deployed for facility defense during the Insurrection. Several Mark II advancements were incorporated into later models, such as an energy-dispersing refractive coating on its plating and automated sealing systems for use in vacuum. Despite producing more models than the original Mark I, most of this generation was mothballed as production quickly shifted to the Mark III.

## MARK III

Although it also was hamstrung by slow development of compact fusion power plants, the Mark III would later prove to be the basis for the large armored defense systems developed by the MJOLNIR's sister project, HRUNTING/YGGDRASIL. Cross-pollination between the two projects has continued over the years, resulting in successful bipedal weapon systems such as the Cyclops and Colossus.

# PROJECT: MJOLNIR

Dr. Halsey adopted the program name "MJOLNIR" for her exoskeleton research. Mjolnir revolutionized mobile armor technology and led to the first viable powered assault armor systems. Mjolnir is notable for its elaborate engineering and precision, each suit was a work of art, hand-tuned for individual Spartans and expected to function in the harshest of environments for months at a time between maintenance and refueling cycles. This reliability and attention to detail comes at an extreme cost in terms of both resources and time required to produce a single suit.

# MARK IV

The first armor line to emerge from the MJOLNIR project was Mark IV, Dr. Halsey's revolutionary powered assault armor that has since been the template for all exoskeleton designs that have followed. Created specifically for Spartan-II supersoldiers, the armor's revolutionary liquid metal musculature and compact fusion reactor was a watershed in powered armor development. Mark IV was a remarkable success for over two decades with constant iterations and development testbeds for newly developed technologies, including early versions of energy shielding.

# MARK V

The last Mjolnir class to be designed by Dr. Halsey, the Mark V incorporated every improvement made to the Mark IV over its decades of service and added two monumental new additions: (1) energy shielding, which had been reverse-engineered from Covenant technology and (2) a neural interface upgrade and crystalline processor lattice capable of carrying a high-order AI construct. The changes were a major shift in Mjolnir's evolution, significantly increasing Spartan survivability and further pushing the potential of man-machine neural interfaces.

# MARK VI

Following shortly after the arrival of Mark V, the release of Mark VI incorporated a handful of seemingly negligible upgrades, though collectively they represent a significant improvement. The Mark VI featured improved energy shielding, refined exoskeleton musculature, and standardized the Mjolnir "plug-in" modules. These improvements were soon incorporated in Generation 2 armor.

# GENERATION 2

Built using a substantially refactored set of technologies compared to the original Mjolnir, GEN2 armor uses a spiral-development model, allowing the UNSC and its various corporate partners to iterate and evolve armor systems much faster and more efficiently than ever before. GEN2 Mjolnir focuses on combining and restructuring all technologies of the previous generations, allowing for cheaper production and simplified integration of specialized software and hardware modules. There are many classes of Generation 2 Mjolnir, designed and manufactured by a large number of corporations who see considerable potential both in the technology and the expanding markets offered by the growing Spartan branch. Those companies that were contracted for Mark V and Mark V production had a substantial head start in this work, but the new architecture proved to be a challenge to fully adopt even by experienced designers.

# COMBAT KNIFE

## SPARTAN CLOSE COMBAT WEAPON

### STATISTICS

MANUFACTURER: WATERSHED DIVISION

IN SERVICE: 2551–PRESENT

WEIGHT: 2 KG (4.4 LB)

LENGTH: 365.8 MM (14.4 IN)

AMMUNITION: N/A

FIRE MODES: N/A

ACTION: MELEE

FEED SYSTEM: N/A

### RATINGS

RANGE 1/10

RATE OF FIRE 1/10

DAMAGE 8/10

RELIABILITY 10/10

HANDLING 10/10

Designed and built for use by Spartans, the hyper-dense metal alloys used to construct the standard M11 knife make it almost unbreakable. When wielded by a Spartan wearing Mjolnir armor, the blade can be thrust with force sufficient to penetrate both energy shielding and hardened armor. Spartans are warned that combat blades are extraordinarily sharp and retain their edge even after repeated use. Mishandling of these weapons may result in serious injury and equipment damage.

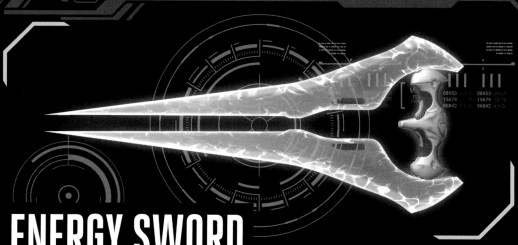

# ENERGY SWORD

## COVENANT PLASMA BLADE

### STATISTICS

MANUFACTURER: ASSEMBLY FORGES

IN SERVICE: N/A

WEIGHT: 2.4 KG (5.3 LB)

LENGTH: 1285 MM (50.6 IN) WHEN ACTIVATED

AMMUNITION: INTERNAL ENERGY CELL

FIRE MODES: N/A

ACTION: PLASMA GENERATOR

FEED SYSTEM: N/A

### RATINGS

RANGE 1/10

RATE OF FIRE 1/10

DAMAGE 10/10

RELIABILITY 7/10

HANDLING 10/10

Elegant and deadly, the Energy Sword is a martial weapon wielded by Sangheili warriors for close-quarters, hand-to-hand combat. The "blade" of the Energy Sword is a confined mass of superheated plasma, generated and shaped by field generators built into the weapon's hilt. Mass-produced models feature a simple hilt design, but those with a long history can become quite ornate after centuries of embellishment.

Variation in the Energy Swords crafting process and quality are expressed in both the shape and the color of the blade. A blade's contours can have either smooth curves or elegant angles, and while most Energy Swords glow with a blue tint, Sangheili special forces have been known to wield blades that blaze red. Smaller, wrist-mounted plasma blades are also used by the Elites of some Covenant fleets, though it remains unclear why these are not used more widely.

# GRAVITY HAMMER

## BRUTE ENERGY MAUL

### STATISTICS

MANUFACTURER: CLAN WORKSHOPS

IN SERVICE: N/A

WEIGHT: 38.7 KG (85.3 LB)

LENGTH: 2037 MM (80.2 IN)

AMMUNITION: INTERNAL ENERGY CELL

FIRE MODES: N/A

ACTION: GRAVITIC IMPELLER

FEED SYSTEM: N/A

### RATINGS

RANGE 1/10

RATE OF FIRE 1/10

DAMAGE 10/10

RELIABILITY 9/10

HANDLING 7/10

Gravity Hammers are symbols of leadership among the Jiralhanae and are wielded only by elite troops and chieftains. Each Gravity Hammer is a combination of Brute and Covenant engineering, with repurposed gravitic impellers integrated into the striking face of a traditional bladed warhammer. The impellers provide additional driving force to each strike and create a kinetic pulse wave on impact, which is powerful enough to displace armored vehicles and shatter reinforced plascrete columns.

# LIGHTBLADE

## FORERUNNER CLOSE COMBAT WEAPON

### STATISTICS

MANUFACTURER: N/A
IN SERVICE: N/A
WEIGHT: N/A
LENGTH: VARIABLE
AMMUNITION: EXTERNAL POWER
FIRE MODES: N/A
ACTION: HARDLIGHT GENERATOR
FEED SYSTEM: N/A

### RATINGS

RANGE 1/10
RATE OF FIRE 1/10
DAMAGE 10/10
RELIABILITY 10/10
HANDLING 8/10

Knights and other Forerunner military constructs are fitted with Lightblade weapons cast from coalesced energy and shaped force shields for use against Flood-parasitized life-forms in close combat. These weapons damage with a combination of heat and force, sterilizing all matter they come into contact with. Impossibly sharp, the Lightblades also have potential applications for human industry and are much safer to operate than shaped-plasma equivalents. Modified Lightblade generators, which can be fitted to standard accessory rails, are now undergoing field testing by Spartans aboard the UNSC *Infinity* and are available for field use.

# INFANTRY WEAPONS

# MAGNUM

## UNSC HEAVY PISTOL

### STATISTICS

MANUFACTURER: MISRIAH ARMORY

IN SERVICE: 2414–PRESENT

WEIGHT: 2.3 KG (5.1 LB)

LENGTH: 347 MM (13.7 IN)

AMMUNITION: 12.7×40MM

FIRE MODES: SEMI-AUTOMATIC

ACTION: SHORT RECOIL OPERATION

FEED SYSTEM: 8-ROUND DETACHABLE BOX MAGAZINE

### RATINGS

RANGE 3/10

RATE OF FIRE 1/10

DAMAGE 3/10

RELIABILITY 10/10

HANDLING 8/10

The M6 Magnum is the standard-issue sidearm for the UNSC. The modernized variant of the M6—the M6H2—features improved Smart Link electronics and an accurized barrel. M6 sidearms issued to Spartan personnel have customized grips and metamaterial film coatings for improved performance in vacuum and corrosive atmospheres. The coating can be altered to "skin" the weapon with custom camouflage patterns and imagery. The standard round for the M6 is semi-armor piercing high-explosive (SAPHE). The Magnum is primarily intended to be a backup weapon and is best employed at short ranges.

# PLASMA PISTOL

## COVENANT DIRECTED ENERGY PISTOL

### STATISTICS

**MANUFACTURER:** ASSEMBLY FORGES

**IN SERVICE:** N/A

**WEIGHT:** 3.5 KG (7.7 LB)

**LENGTH:** 369 MM (14.5 IN)

**AMMUNITION:** SHAPED PLASMA

**FIRE MODES:** SEMI-AUTOMATIC, OVERCHARGE

**ACTION:** PLASMA GENERATOR

**FEED SYSTEM:** 100-SHOT PULSED POWER CELL

### RATINGS

**RANGE** 3/10

**RATE OF FIRE** 1/10

**DAMAGE** 5/10

**RELIABILITY** 7/10

**HANDLING** 7/10

The Plasma Pistol was the standard sidearm for Covenant infantry, and it remains the most widely used and versatile weapon in known space. It is simple to use and requires almost no maintenance, which makes it an attractive weapon for both Covenant successor factions and human criminals. The internal battery can be recharged using many different power sources, including UNSC generators, if adapters are available.

The Plasma Pistol can fire either rapid pulses of superheated plasma or an overcharged plasma bolt that can disable vehicles and overload shield generators. Overcharged shots and extended firing build up enormous amounts of heat, which must be periodically vented to avoid a catastrophic malfunction. Personnel are warned to not place exposed skin or flammable objects near the venting ports.

# ASSAULT RIFLE

## UNSC INFANTRY LONGARM

### STATISTICS

**MANUFACTURER:** MISRIAH ARMORY
**IN SERVICE:** 2395–PRESENT
**WEIGHT:** 3.5 KG (7.7 LB)
**LENGTH:** 999 MM (39.4 IN)
**AMMUNITION:** 7.62×51MM
**FIRE MODES:** SEMI-AUTOMATIC, AUTOMATIC
**ACTION:** GAS OPERATED, ROTATING BOLT
**FEED SYSTEM:** 32-ROUND DETACHABLE BOX MAGAZINE

### RATINGS

**RANGE** 4/10
**RATE OF FIRE** 8/10
**DAMAGE** 5/10
**RELIABILITY** 10/10
**HANDLING** 6/10

Reliable and easy to use, the MA5 represents the oldest rifle platform currently employed by the UNSC, with more than a dozen variations still in use. The MA5D model is standard-issue for Spartans, and can be configured with various combat optics and accessories to optimize for specific tactical situations. Those issued to Spartans include the same protective metamaterial coating used on the M6H2 Magnum.

The standard round for the MA5 is armor-piercing (AP). Specialist ammunition is available by request.

# PLASMA RIFLE

## COVENANT DIRECTED ENERGY RIFLE

### STATISTICS

MANUFACTURER: ASSEMBLY FORGES

IN SERVICE: N/A

WEIGHT: 5.9 KG (13 LB)

LENGTH: 621 MM (24.4 IN)

AMMUNITION: SHAPED PLASMA

FIRE MODES: AUTOMATIC

ACTION: PLASMA GENERATOR

FEED SYSTEM: 100-SHOT PULSED POWER CELL

### RATINGS

RANGE 5/10

RATE OF FIRE 7/10

DAMAGE 7/10

RELIABILITY 6/10

HANDLING 6/10

Plasma Rifles were the signature weapon of the Covenant's Sangheili warriors for centuries. With the loss of High Charity and its primary Assembly Forges, the rifle has become rarer, but limited production continues at the moons of Sanghelios, Hesduros, and on Doisac. The Plasma Rifle's distinctive silhouette is the result of its two generator subassemblies placed above and below the trigger assembly, creating a streamlined shape vaguely reminiscent of a predator animal's claw. The generators fire in sequence, discharging superheated plasma from the charging and accelerator poles.

Though extremely efficient, a significant amount of waste heat is produced while firing, forcing the wielder to fire short, controlled bursts or risk overheating. Overheating triggers a safety cutoff and cooling cycle. The heat and ejected plasma produced during this venting process can cause severe burns.

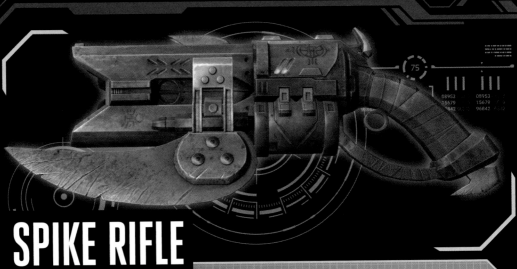

# SPIKE RIFLE

## BRUTE SIDEARM

### STATISTICS

MANUFACTURER: CLAN WORKSHOPS

IN SERVICE: N/A

WEIGHT: 7 KG (15.4 LB)

LENGTH: 817 MM (32.2 IN)

AMMUNITION: SPIKE BOLTS

FIRE MODES: AUTOMATIC

ACTION: GRAVITIC ACCELERATOR

FEED SYSTEM: 40-ROUND DETACHABLE DRUM MAGAZINE

### RATINGS

RANGE 5/10

RATE OF FIRE 8/10

DAMAGE 6/10

RELIABILITY 4/10

HANDLING 7/10

The Spike Rifle is a fully automatic, drum-fed, double-barreled Jiralhanae weapon, which uses repurposed gravity slings to accelerate semi-molten armor-piercing projectiles at high velocity. The weapon resembles a large revolver with two large bayonets mounted diagonally along the barrel. The key ring trigger is simple, but the pull weight can prove an issue for unaugmented personnel. As with all Brute weapons, there is no safety—once the Spike Rifle has a magazine inserted it is ready to fire.

Ammunition is loaded from sealed, disposable magazine canisters holding a small power supply and 40 bolts. The spike ammunition is coated with a pyrophoric compound unique to Doisac, which burns with a white-hot intensity once exposed to atmospheric oxygen. Even Jiralhanae do not attempt to handle rounds without protective gloves.

# SUPPRESSOR

## FORERUNNER DEFENSIVE WEAPON

### STATISTICS

MANUFACTURER: UNKNOWN

IN SERVICE: N/A

WEIGHT: 11 KG (24.3 LB)

LENGTH: 942 MM (37.1 IN)

AMMUNITION: HARD LIGHT SPLINTER

FIRE MODES: AUTOMATIC

ACTION: FIELD EFFECTOR

FEED SYSTEM: 48-SHOT DETACHABLE ENERGY CELL

### RATINGS

RANGE 5/10

RATE OF FIRE 6/10

DAMAGE 5/10

RELIABILITY 10/10

HANDLING 8/10

First encountered equipping Forerunner Knight constructs on the shield world of Requiem, the Suppressor is a portable, rapid-fire infantry weapon that ejects target-seeking high-velocity hard light shards as its primary projectile. These shards do damage through have a mix of kinetic and thermal effects and appear to be intended for use against Flood biomass. Additional details on the function and capabilities of these devices are the subject of ongoing research.

Examples of these weapons recovered after the Requiem conflict have revealed substantial evolution of its internal mechanisms and fire control settings. It is possible this is an adaptive function of the weapon itself, as other Forerunner weapons have also demonstrated target-optimization routines.

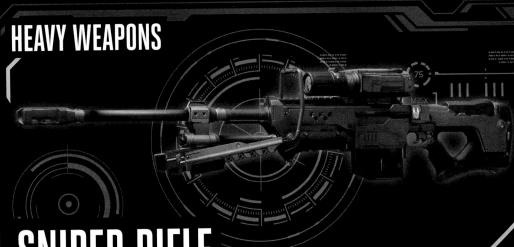

# SNIPER RIFLE

## UNSC ANTI-MATERIEL RIFLE

### STATISTICS

MANUFACTURER: MISRIAH ARMORY

IN SERVICE: 2460–PRESENT

WEIGHT: 14.5 KG (32 LB)

LENGTH: 1612 MM (63.5 IN)

AMMUNITION: 14.5 MM×114 MM

FIRE MODES: SEMI-AUTOMATIC

ACTION: RECOIL-OPERATED, ROTATING BOLT

FEED SYSTEM: 4-ROUND DETACHABLE BOX MAGAZINE

### RATINGS

RANGE 8/10

RATE OF FIRE 1/10

DAMAGE 10/10

RELIABILITY 10/10

HANDLING 6/10

Adopted by the entire UNSC in 2521, the Sniper Rifle System 99 (SRS99) family of long-range rifles has had a distinguished career through decades of conflict, acquiring a reputation for power and accuracy in environments ranging from the vacuum of space to underwater. Though bulky and cumbersome for unaugmented soldiers, Spartans routinely land accurate shots with the weapon at over a kilometer range, while on the move, due to their strength and the Mjolnir's VISR link.

Standard ammunition for UNSC Sniper Rifles is armor-piercing fin-stabilized discarding sabot (APFSDS), which can defeat most Covenant infantry in a single shot and inflict substantial damage to lightly armored vehicles.

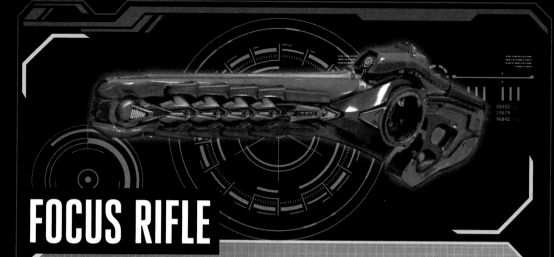

# FOCUS RIFLE

## COVENANT SPECIAL PURPOSE RIFLE

### STATISTICS

MANUFACTURER: ASSEMBLY FORGES

IN SERVICE: N/A

WEIGHT: 17.1 KG (37.7 LB)

LENGTH: 1452 MM (57.2 IN)

AMMUNITION: FOCUSED PLASMA

FIRE MODES: CONTINUOUS FIRE/BEAM

ACTION: PLASMA GENERATOR

FEED SYSTEM: 100-SHOT PULSED POWER CELL

### RATINGS

RANGE 8/10

RATE OF FIRE 1/10

DAMAGE 10/10

RELIABILITY 10/10

HANDLING 6/10

The Focus Rifle is a sniper-style weapon that projects electromagnetically guided streams of superheated plasma that can be precisely tuned for either range or power. The Focus Rifle copies some elements of the sterilization beams fitted to Aggressor Sentinels, but the magnetic accelerators and particle guide beam emitter are novel creations not seen in any Forerunner design. The inventive features of this weapon, and seeming improvements over original Forerunner design, represent a counterpoint to the prevailing opinion that the Covenant lacked innovative thinking when it came to technology.

The targeting protocols for the Focus Rifle are unusual, and incompatible with most interlink translation software. While Spartans can make effective use of Focus Rifles, only Sangheili and Kig-Yar marksman systems currently allow precise adjustment of plasma beam angle for semi-automatic target tracking.

# ROCKET LAUNCHER

## UNSC DESTRUCTIVE DEVICE

### STATISTICS

MANUFACTURER: MISRIAH ARMORY

IN SERVICE: 2481–PRESENT

WEIGHT: 10.8 KG (23.8 LB)

LENGTH: 1406 MM (55.4 IN)

AMMUNITION: 102 MM ROCKET

FIRE MODES: SEMIAUTOMATIC

ACTION: REVOLVER

FEED SYSTEM: 2-ROUND DETACHABLE MAGAZINE

### RATINGS

RANGE 8/10

RATE OF FIRE 1/10

DAMAGE 10/10

RELIABILITY 10/10

HANDLING 6/10

The M41 SPNKr rocket launcher is among the most powerful man-portable heavy weapons in the UNSC inventory. Although its bulky, twin-tube launcher configuration can be challenging to carry, the launcher's ability to fire two high-explosive shaped warheads in quick succession is often a critical factor in disabling or destroying Covenant vehicles protected by both energy shielding and heavy armor.

The standard M41 ammunition package is a pair of M19 unguided rockets with multi-purpose high-explosive shaped charge (HESC) warheads. Other options are available by special requisition for Spartans, including guided missiles and hunter-killer loitering munitions.

# FUEL ROD CANNON

## COVENANT EXPLOSIVE PROJECTILE LAUNCHER

### STATISTICS

MANUFACTURER: ASSEMBLY FORGES

IN SERVICE: N/A

WEIGHT: 20.8 KG (45.9 LB)

LENGTH: 1406 MM (55.4 IN)

AMMUNITION: 38 MM FUEL RODS

FIRE MODES: SEMIAUTOMATIC

ACTION: SELF-LOADING

FEED SYSTEM: 5-ROUND DETACHABLE MAGAZINE

### RATINGS

RANGE 7/10

RATE OF FIRE 2/10

DAMAGE 9/10

RELIABILITY 9/10

HANDLING 6/10

Fuel Rod Cannons are portable heavy weapons developed by the Covenant and now widely used by several alien factions in both anti-armor and antipersonnel roles. Only examples manufactured since 2552 can be closely analyzed or used by Spartans, as they lack a set of crucial security interlocks, which trigger a self-destruct if opened or picked up by unapproved personnel. Fuel rods fire in a parabolic arc, flaring up after leaving the launcher, and detonate on impact. Effective range and blast radius varies widely, based on the quality and instability of fuel rods being used.

UNSC personnel are warned that fuel rod ammunition is both radioactive and extremely toxic. Spartans should never handle fuel rod components without wearing Mjolnir armor.

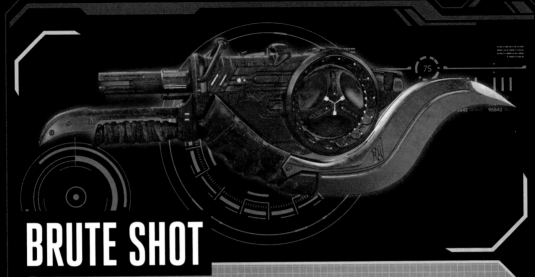

# BRUTE SHOT

## BRUTE GRENADE LAUNCHER

### STATISTICS

MANUFACTURER: CLAN WORKSHOPS

IN SERVICE: N/A

WEIGHT: 19 KG (42 LB)

LENGTH: 1811 MM (71.3 IN)

AMMUNITION: 52 MM GRENADE

FIRE MODES: SEMIAUTOMATIC

ACTION: BLOWBACK

FEED SYSTEM: 6-ROUND INTERNAL MAGAZINE

### RATINGS

RANGE 7/10

RATE OF FIRE 4/10

DAMAGE 6/10

RELIABILITY 3/10

HANDLING 6/10

The Brute Shot is a Jiralhanae-designed projectile weapon that is most closely analogous to a UNSC automatic grenade launcher but with a large stock-mounted blade for close-quarters combat. Jiralhanae use the weapon in a direct assault role, firing grenades at close range to disrupt the enemy as shock troops charge into melee range. Ammunition is supplied in belts of three to six grenades, which are fed into the weapon's internal magazine with an autoloader.

Standard ammunition uses a high-explosive concussion (HEC) warhead. The Brute Shot itself lacks a weapon safety, but its grenades are almost completely inert until primed in the firing chamber. This safety feature appears to be a Covenant modification and may be missing on newly manufactured ammunition. Spartans are warned that all Brute munitions and weapon systems should be handled with extreme care.

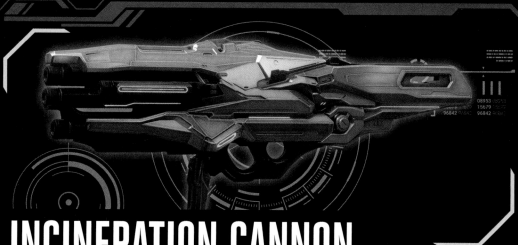

# INCINERATION CANNON

## FORERUNNER PARTICLE CANNON

### STATISTICS

MANUFACTURER: UNKNOWN

IN SERVICE: N/A

WEIGHT: 20.7 KG (45.6 LB)

LENGTH: 1348 MM (53.1 IN)

AMMUNITION: PARTICLE CASCADE

FIRE MODES: BURST, CHARGED SHOT

ACTION: PULSED POWER

FEED SYSTEM: 6-SHOT RECHARGEABLE POWER CELL

### RATINGS

RANGE 7/10

RATE OF FIRE 4/10

DAMAGE 6/10

RELIABILITY 10/10

HANDLING 6/10

The Incineration Cannon was first encountered as the primary armament of Forerunner combat machines associated with the Promethean forces on Requiem. Functionally similar to a UNSC rocket launcher, the Incineration Cannon fires two to five packets of highly unstable energy from its twin barrels, which may release secondary charges on impact. The configuration of these weapons is highly variable, though only minimal control of the weapon can be exerted through the Mjolnir's Smart Link conversion/interpreter software. Contact your armorer for details on the Incineration Cannons in the inventory, which are available for use.

Energy cells compatible with the Incineration Cannon are controlled access items due to their high energy density. Handle these items with the same safety considerations as live warheads.

# GROUND VEHICLES

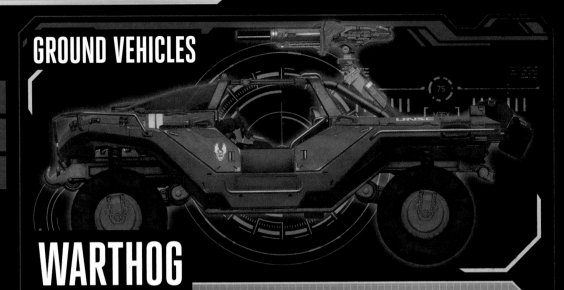

# WARTHOG

## UNSC FORCE APPLICATION VEHICLE

### STATISTICS

MANUFACTURER: AMG TRANSPORT DYNAMICS

IN SERVICE: 2319–PRESENT

CREW: 1 DRIVER + 1 PASSENGER + 1 GUNNER

COMBAT WEIGHT: 3 TONNES (3.25 TONS)

LENGTH: 6300 MM (20.5 FT)

WIDTH: 3000 MM (9.8 FT)

HEIGHT: 2500 MM (8.1 FT)

ARMAMENT: 1×M49 VULCAN L/AAG

SPEED: 125 KM/H (78 MPH)

### RATINGS

FIREPOWER 4/10

ARMOR 2/10

HANDLING 8/10

RESILIENCE 6/10

The basic Warthog chassis has been in UEG service for over two centuries, and the latest M12B model continues the vehicle's proud tradition of service into the post–Covenant War era. Numerous variants of the Warthog are in service, including dedicated troop transport and mobile repair bay, but the versatile Light Reconnaissance Vehicle (LRV) with a M343A2 or M49 chaingun is the most common. The Warthogs' widespread use means that every UNSC soldier is familiar with their operation, and they are an integral part of many Spartan missions.

Though originally designed to provide close defense against enemy aircraft and drones, the Warthog's chaingun also has an anti-infantry and anti-light armor use, and Spartans should become familiar with this tactical role. Standard ammunition loadout for the weapon is armor piercing, but proximity-fused high-explosive, less-than-lethal stunballs, or other specialist rounds can be made available for use.

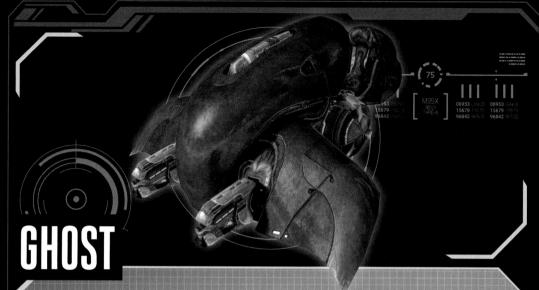

# GHOST

## COVENANT SCOUT

### STATISTICS

MANUFACTURER: ASSEMBLY FORGES

IN SERVICE: N/A

CREW: 1 DRIVER

COMBAT WEIGHT: 0.5 TONNES (0.55 TONS)

LENGTH: 4200 MM (13.8 FT)

WIDTH: 3900 MM (12.6 FT)

HEIGHT: 1800 MM (6 FT)

ARMAMENT: 2×LIGHT PLASMA CANNON

SPEED: 132 KM/H (82 MPH)

### RATINGS

FIREPOWER 5/10

ARMOR 4/10

HANDLING 9/10

RESILIENCE 6/10

The Ghost is the Covenant's premiere scouting vehicle, and it remains a very common vehicle among alien forces. Rebels and criminal elements on several UEG worlds have also begun to make use of the vehicle, and all UNSC forces have standing orders to recover these vehicles for ONI analysis. Though many variants of the Ghost exist, they all use a boosted-gravity propulsion system, which has the advantages of a hovercraft and few of the disadvantages. Ghost variants adapted for long-range endurance and patrols feature large power cells near the engine's primary motivator; Spartan marksmen are advised that these components are highly volatile and only lightly armored.

Ghosts are armed with dual rapid-fire plasma cannons, but many Covenant drivers have displayed a preference for using the vehicle as a ram in close-range encounters. Although risky, baiting a Ghost driver to attempt a ram, and then initiating a hijack, may be an effective strategy in some situations.

# SCORPION

## UNSC MAIN BATTLE TANK

### STATISTICS

**MANUFACTURER:** CHALYBS DEFENSE SOLUTIONS

**IN SERVICE:** 2218–PRESENT

**CREW:** 1 OPERATOR

**COMBAT WEIGHT:** 59.9 TONNES (66 TONS)

**SPEED:** 48 KM/H (30 MPH)

**ARMAMENT:** 1×90 MM CANNON, 1×7.62 MM MACHINE GUN

**LENGTH:** 8900 MM (29.2 FT)

**WIDTH:** 7000 MM (23 FT)

**HEIGHT:** 4100 MM (13.5 FT)

### RATINGS

**FIREPOWER** 9/10

**ARMOR** 8/10

**HANDLING** 3/10

**RESILIENCE** 8/10

The Scorpion's rugged, adaptable design has changed little from its origins at the dawn of human interstellar colonization. Several models remain in service with the UNSC and planetary defense forces. Though they vary in size, mass, and armament, all feature a heavily armored main hull, unmanned turret, and four independent track pods. The M808B model is among the most common variant, due a combination of affordability, simplicity, and versatility.

Apart from some specialized variants, the Scorpion is configured as a main battle tank, with a large cannon and secondary machine gun as offensive systems. Spartans are cautioned that Mjolnir armor and shields are not rated to withstand 90 mm cannon impacts and caution should always be exercised in situations where enemy forces have access to these vehicles.

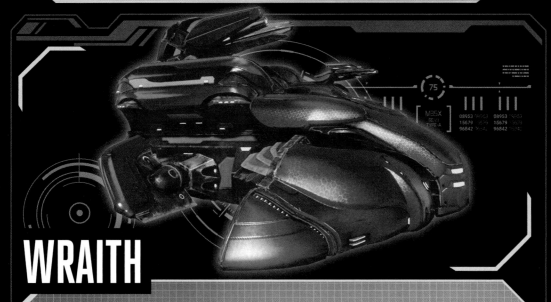

# WRAITH

## COVENANT MORTAR TANK

## STATISTICS

**MANUFACTURER:** ASSEMBLY FORGES

**IN SERVICE:** N/A

**CREW:** 1 DRIVER + 1 GUNNER

**COMBAT WEIGHT:** 42.3 TONNES (46.6 TONS)

**SPEED:** 82 KM/H (51 MPH)

**ARMAMENT:** 1×PLASMA MORTAR, 1×LIGHT PLASMA CANNON

**LENGTH:** 8800 MM (29 FT)

**WIDTH:** 9200 MM (30.1 FT)

**HEIGHT:** 3800 MM (12.5 FT)

## RATINGS

**FIREPOWER** 9/10

**ARMOR** 8/10

**HANDLING** 7/10

**RESILIENCE** 8/10

With a distinctively aggressive design, the Wraith is one of the most recognizable Covenant vehicles currently in use and is considered a significant threat to most enemies who encounter it. Armed with a devastating plasma mortar that can shatter even heavily reinforced defenses from long distances, the Wraith tank is lethal at range. Despite the Wraith's large size, its boosted-gravity drive allows for impressive speed and surprisingly agile maneuvers over most terrain, including water.

The Banished and Covenant successor factions make extensive use of custom loadouts and modifications to the base Wraith chassis, and Spartans are expected to carefully observe and report any new variants they encounter in the field.

# MAMMOTH

## UNSC MOBILE BASE CENTER

## STATISTICS

MANUFACTURER: ACHERON SECURITY

IN SERVICE: 2553–PRESENT

CREW: 3 CREW + 30 PASSENGERS

COMBAT WEIGHT: 439 TONNES (483.9 TONS)

SPEED: 74 KM/H (46 MPH)

ARMAMENT: 1×350 MM MAGNETIC ACCELERATOR CANNON, 2×65 MM MLRS

LENGTH: 68300 MM (224.1 FT)

WIDTH: 32800 MM (107.6 FT)

HEIGHT: 27100 MM (89 FT)

## RATINGS

FIREPOWER 10/10

ARMOR 10/10

HANDLING 1/10

RESILIENCE 10/10

The M510 Mammoth is the largest ground vehicle currently used by the UNSC, operating as a mobile forward operating center and siege machine. Adapted from expeditionary machines used on UEG colony words, the Mammoth can store and service smaller vehicles in its internal cargo bay and provide heavy fire support against ground, air, and even orbital targets, with its heavy railgun.

# SCARAB

## COVENANT EXCAVATOR

## STATISTICS

MANUFACTURER: ASSEMBLY FORGES

IN SERVICE: N/A

CREW: 1 SUPERVISOR + 12 PASSENGERS

COMBAT WEIGHT: 171.8 TONNES (189.4 TONS)

SPEED: 76 KM/H (47 MPH)

ARMAMENT: 1×ULTRAHEAVY

FOCUS CANNON

LENGTH: 48600 MM (159.5 FT)

WIDTH: 48300 MM (158.5 FT)

HEIGHT: 38700 MM (127 FT)

## RATINGS

FIREPOWER 10/10

ARMOR 8/10

HANDLING 3/10

RESILIENCE 10/10

Scarabs are large, heavily armored all-terrain walkers employed by the Covenant and Banished as mobile bases, combat engineering vehicles, artifact excavators, and heavy weapon platforms. Though the Scarab does have a crew, and a command deck in which they direct the platform, primary control is in the hands of the Lekgolo ("Hunter worm") meta-colony distributed throughout the structure, with a central node located near the primary reactor. The crew provides direction and helps manage the various systems, but ultimately the Scarab can operate completely autonomously.

The Scarab is among the most dangerous threats that a Spartan can encounter, and they should never be engaged directly. Look for opportunities to board the vehicle and either eliminate the supervisor or attack the control colony directly to trigger a self-destruct.

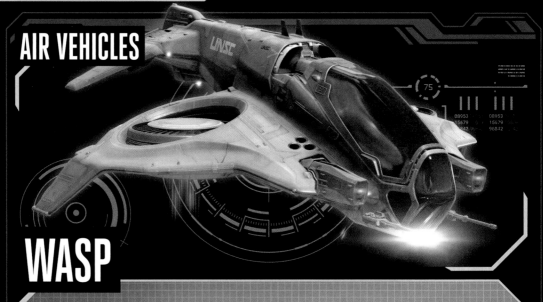

# WASP

## UNSC ATTACK VTOL

### STATISTICS

MANUFACTURER: MISRIAH ARMORY

IN SERVICE: 2553–PRESENT

CREW: 1 PILOT

COMBAT WEIGHT: 1360.7 KG (3000 LB)

SPEED: 500 KM/H (311 MPH) TOP SPEED

ARMAMENT: 2×7.62 MM HEAVY MACHINE GUN, 2×50 MM MISSILE LAUNCHERS

LENGTH: 7620 MM (25 FT)

WIDTH: 6400.8 MM (21 FT)

HEIGHT: 2225 MM (7.3 FT)

### RATINGS

FIREPOWER 6/10

ARMOR 2/10

HANDLING 9/10

RESILIENCE 3/10

The Wasp is a one-man strike VTOL currently undergoing field trials with the UNSC. Using powerful ducted fan engines for lift, the Wasp is surprisingly nimble and can reach mission areas quickly with the use of air-cooled vectored-thrust fusion thrusters in forward flight. Current operational doctrine is to use the Wasp in either as gunship escort for troop transports or on-call close air support for special forces teams.

The Spartan branch has been asked to assess its tactical utility for our specific needs, and you can test the vehicle in War Games or review prototypes manufactured in the *Infinity*'s onboard factory module on Hangar A-6.

Wasps can be broken down for shipping in compact storage containers, and reassembled with minimal tools. Though not currently a training requirement, Commander Palmer has strongly suggested all *Infinity* Spartans become familiar with the assembly process.

# BANSHEE

## COVENANT ATTACK FLYER

## STATISTICS

MANUFACTURER: ASSEMBLY FORGES

IN SERVICE: N/A

CREW: 1 PILOT

COMBAT WEIGHT: 1.2 TONNES (1.3 TONS)

SPEED: 108 KM/H (67 MPH) LOITERING MODE

ARMAMENT: 2×LIGHT PLASMA CANNONS, 1×FUEL ROD CANNON

LENGTH: 7100 MM (23.2 FT)

WIDTH: 7500 MM (24.6 FT)

HEIGHT: 3600 MM (11.8 FT)

## RATINGS

FIREPOWER 6/10

ARMOR 4/10

HANDLING 9/10

RESILIENCE 6/10

The Banshee's ease of operation, reliability, maneuverability, and armament make it highly sought on the interstellar arms market. The Banshee is controlled by a single operator, who lies prone on the sled-like control couch to access the vehicle's control panel. Entrance is from the rear of the vehicle, and the bulbous nose section hinges open to allow easy access. Your Mjolnir suit incorporates the latest Covenant control harness emulators and software exploit package, which can unlock any Banshees you encounter in the field.

Note that the Banshee's pilot's compartment is not sealed and the few have any form of life-support hookup. An integral gravitic compensation system shields the pilot from maneuvering-induced stresses, but it should be noted that the Banshee does not feature ejection seats or other safety equipment mandated on UNSC vehicles.

# PELICAN

## UNSC COMBAT DROPSHIP

### STATISTICS

MANUFACTURER: MISRIAH ARMORY

IN SERVICE: 2392–PRESENT

CREW: 3 CREW + 14 PASSENGERS

COMBAT WEIGHT: 77 TONNES (89.9 TONS)

SPEED: 900 KM/H (559 MPH)

LOITERING MODE

ARMAMENT: 1×70 MM CANNON,
4×WEAPON HARDPOINTS

LENGTH: 31200 MM (102.4 FT)

WIDTH: 25500 MM (83.7 FT)

HEIGHT: 10700 MM (35 FT)

### RATINGS

FIREPOWER 4/10

ARMOR 6/10

HANDLING 5/10

RESILIENCE 7/10

The Pelican is the UNSC's standard troop dropship used for orbit-to-surface and surface-to-surface transportation of infantry and armored vehicles. The D77 is the most ubiquitous variant and is widely marketed to police, security, corporate, and civilian markets. The Pelican can transport up to twenty-four seated passengers in the cargo bay and carry a vehicle mounted to the external hardpoint clamp.

# PHANTOM

## COVENANT ASSAULT DROPSHIP

### STATISTICS

MANUFACTURER: ASSEMBLY FORGES

IN SERVICE: N/A

CREW: 2 CREW + 20 PASSENGERS

COMBAT WEIGHT: 59 TONNES (3.25 TONS)

SPEED: 965.6 KM/H (600 MPH)

LOITERING MODE

ARMAMENT: 1×HEAVY PLASMA CANNON,
2×LIGHT PLASMA CANNON

LENGTH: 33200 MM (109 FT)

WIDTH: 20100 MM (65.9 FT)

HEIGHT: 12600 MM (41.2 FT)

### RATINGS

FIREPOWER 9/10

ARMOR 8/10

HANDLING 3/10

RESILIENCE 8/10

Covenant records indicate that some form of Phantom has been in Covenant service for millennia as troop transports, cargo shuttles, and personal chariots for the Prophets. The cockpit for the Phantom is an armored pod accessed from the troop bay. Holographic controls and displays feed in information from outside the craft—as with most Covenant vehicles, the Phantom does not have viewports.

The troop bay is accessed either through the rear hatch or flank doors, but most find it more convenient to use the dropship's integral gravity lift. At maximum capacity the troop bay can hold thirty warriors, with one or two armored vehicles carried below the vehicle in a gravity sling.

BE VIGILANT. WE LIVE IN A DANGEROUS NEW AGE WHERE THE SPECTERS OF BATTLES FOUGHT NOT ONLY YEARS AGO BUT EONS AGO ARE RISING TO STRIKE. IF HUMANITY IS TO SURVIVE, SPARTANS ARE THE WEAPONS THAT WILL PROTECT US AND OUR INTERESTS FOR GENERATIONS TO COME. YOU KNOW YOUR DUTY. UNDERTAKE IT WITH HONOR.

GOOD LUCK.